BARBARA PHINNEY
FATAL SECRETS

Steeple
Hill®

Published by Steeple Hill Books™

Special thanks and acknowledgment to Barbara Phinney for her contribution to the Protecting the Witnesses miniseries.

STEEPLE HILL BOOKS

Steeple Hill®

Recycling programs for this product may not exist in your area.

ISBN-13: 978-0-373-44393-2

FATAL SECRETS

Copyright © 2010 by Harlequin Books S.A.

www.SteepleHill.com

Printed in U.S.A.

Kristin's heart swelled in sympathy for Zane.

They were both searching for their family. In a way, she'd found a kindred spirit. "I'm sorry, Zane."

"It's all right. I've built a good business here in Montana, and searching for my brother is something I do when I have the time. I have even less information on him than you have on your mother so I always knew I might never find him."

"So you're back to square one now?"

"I have one much weaker lead out there, but I'm not expecting anything to come of it. Like I said, I may never find him."

He watched her as if he was also looking for understanding. Her heart lurched. He was hurt, too. He was struggling to find a connection with his past. And like her, he might never find his family.

* * *

PROTECTING THE WITNESSES:

New identities, looming danger and forever love in the Witness Protection Program.

Books by Barbara Phinney

Love Inspired Suspense

Desperate Rescue
Keeping Her Safe
Deadly Homecoming
Fatal Secrets

BARBARA PHINNEY

was born in England and raised in Canada. She has traveled throughout her life, loving to explore the various countries and cultures of the world. After she retired from the Canadian Armed Forces, Barbara turned her hand to romance writing. The thrill of adventure and the love of happy endings, coupled with a too-active imagination, have merged to help her create this and other wonderful stories. Barbara spends her days writing, building her dream home with her husband and enjoying their fast-growing children.

With God we will gain the victory,
and he will trample down our enemies.
—*Psalms* 60:12

PROLOGUE

MEMO: Top Secret
TO: FBI Organized Crime Division; U.S.
    Marshal's Office
FROM: Jackson McGraw, Special Agent in
      Charge, Chicago Field Office, Federal
      Bureau of Investigation
DATE: May 10, 2010
RE: Operation Black Veil

Vincent Martino has escaped custody. We have
received new information from our "Martino
Mystery Witness." Vincent Martino has discovered Eloise Hill's daughter lives in Montana. He
knows her first name only and he is now
believed to be in Montana searching for both
mother and daughter. Salvatore Martino is dying
and the family is stepping up efforts to find
both women.

All police services have been informed.

The Marshal's Office is requested to ensure
all women in the Witness Protection Program
in Montana who fit Eloise's description are pro-

tected. The investigation is continuing on all fronts, including previous deaths, and the daughter (location on a need-to-know basis only) will be informed and told to stay vigilant. Protective custody not required at this time.

Contact SAC McGraw with any information that could assist the FBI in its case against the Martino crime family.

ONE

Nothing is harder than leaving my precious baby girl.

For the past five months, Kristin Perry had hung on to the words her birth mother wrote to FBI agent Jackson McGraw all those years ago. Written just before she'd left.

Eloise Hill was out there somewhere, and in her note to Jackson, she'd said she loved Kristin enough to give her up to keep her safe, something in which Kristin should find comfort.

Comfort didn't come easily, though, Kristin decided as she sat in the café and fought back the first sign of tears. Her new identity, as both orphan *and* adoptee, was still sinking in, displacing any comfort. She'd lost both her adopted parents five months ago, and the ache inside had yet to ease. Only after discovering the contents of her father's safe did she learn of her adopted status. She'd found her real birth certificate, and a note from her birth mother.

But visiting Jackson McGraw, the man to whom her mother had written, had done nothing to solve the mystery of where the woman might be. His last contact with her had been the note Kristin had since memorized.

Dear Jackson:

Nothing I've done, from testifying against a Mafia kingpin, to starting over in the Witness Protection Program, is harder than leaving my precious baby girl. Kristin almost died because of the path I've needed to take. I love her too much to risk her life. For her safety, I must give her up, though it breaks my heart. Please see to it she's placed in a loving, Christian home.

Yours,

Eloise.

Kristin lingered over and over such parts as "nothing is harder" and "breaks my heart." And each time, the ache increased. She needed to find her mother. Her only family now. Or did she now have brothers, sisters?

The mere thought of a big family gripped Kristin. She'd been an only child, with grandparents that were now just a faint memory to her. When her aging parents, Anna and Barton Perry, had died in that terrible car crash last January, she felt so alone.

Not so much now, though. She had a mother somewhere, and while sitting in this downtown coffee shop near her Westbrook, Montana, university campus, watching one particular man enter, Kristin knew she was that much closer to finding her.

Was that Zane Black, the man she'd asked to meet her this Monday morning? With a demeanor that spoke of control, the man threw open the door and strode into the café. He really didn't look as if he belonged in her small town, despite the jeans and sheepskin jacket. Maybe a big city or even Kalispell just south of here, but not in little Westbrook.

Was this the private investigator she'd called? Kristin was about to stand when her cell phone rang, the soft version of "Ein Kleine Nachtmusik" barely heard in the busy café. Turning away from the man, she answered it.

On the other end was an unexpected caller, Jackson McGraw. "I—I was just thinking of you," she said to him shyly.

"Really? Kristin, I have something that needs your attention."

Hope flared in her. "You've found my mother?"

A distinct pause followed. "No. I'm sorry. I've told you all I know. I haven't learned anything new since that day I last saw your mother. She left that night."

Sagging, Kristin raked her fingers through her hair, then quickly smoothed the right side down carefully, as she always did. Beneath the straight brown hair that was cut in such a way to conceal it, lay a thick scar, long and white, devoid of hair. Jackson had told her how she acquired the scar, but for now, she set that thought aside.

"I wish I had better news for you."

Disappointment bit at her, and she blinked back the subsequent tears. "Then why are you calling? I got the impression that we wouldn't contact each other again because Witness Protection made everything too dangerous."

"It does, Kristin. I personally have no access to the program. It belongs to the Department of Justice and the U.S. Marshal's Office. Organized crime investigation comes under my jurisdiction. But I've received some new information that you need to know."

"What is it?" She had nothing to do with organized crime. And her biological mother had been hidden for years, after testifying against one Mafia member.

"It seems that the Martino family has learned you live

in Montana. We believe that they are searching for you."
His words sounded guarded, as if he weighed each one
carefully to ensure a balance of gentleness and warning.

"You mean that man my mother testified against?"

"I mean the whole crime family. As a tribute to Salvatore Martino, the rest of the Martino family and their associates want to get to your mother, but we believe that they want you, too. Or they want you to lead them to your mother. Or both."

She gasped, hunkered over the phone further and set her forehead into her left palm. "I don't understand. Why would they be after me?"

"Hurt you, hurt your mother. They're looking to honor Salvatore Martino, not to make any sense. What we need you to do is stop your search for your mother. We believe it may have sparked some interest in you."

Tears welled up again, causing a knot to tighten around her throat. She couldn't look for her mother? It didn't seem fair. "How do they know I'm in Montana?"

"We're not sure yet. They've learned that your mother gave you up for adoption and that you live in Montana. They know your first name was Kristin years ago, but that's all they know."

Her heart tripped slightly. "Do you think they'd break in to your office and steal my address?"

"No, they won't," he answered tersely. "Even if they could break in, they wouldn't find it because last night I shredded all the info I had on you."

So he must have committed her phone number to memory. So much to do for just her, she thought. Why?

"But if they've discovered you're in Montana," he continued, "they could find out more."

She gasped. "Then they could find my mother, too!"

"Not if I can help it." The grit in his words abraded through her cell phone. He'd do anything, she realized. Odd to have such determination, but since Jackson was the only FBI agent she'd ever met, maybe they were all that dogged. He just seemed so…concerned for her and her mother.

She lifted her head and straightened. "So what should I do? I want to find my mother. I *need* to find her. I have no one," she said, her voice cracking. The wounds of her parents' deaths were still too raw. It had only been four and a half months. "And I…just don't want to go through my life with no one. Do you understand?"

Jackson McGraw didn't speak right away. But when his answer came, his voice had softened. "I do understand. But for now, I need you to trust me, Kristin. Someone is after you, too, and if that person or persons find you, they may wait until you've located your mother. Or they may not wait and hope your death draws *out* your mother."

There was static on the line. "I'm stuck in Chicago right now and can't get out to see you in person, nor do I want to just yet, for your own safety. I'm asking you to suspend your search. Information is being leaked out to the Martino family, so I wouldn't trust anyone at this point. I mean no one."

"But no one here knows I'm adopted, not even the man who opened the safe for me. There are a few older people in Billings, but that's it. Really, only you and your brother know."

She paused, her thoughts skittering from Jackson to Micah McGraw, his younger brother who she'd first contacted because he was a U.S. Marshal in Billings. He'd introduced her to Jackson. Then her thoughts moved to the private investigator she'd hired. All she'd said to Zane

Black was she was looking for a woman. She'd planned to explain everything when she met him today. But now, considering what Jackson had said…should she even say anything at all?

"I'm working as fast as I can to locate your mother, Kristin," Jackson continued, "but in the meantime, please be very vigilant and don't say a word to anyone, not even the police. Not just for your own sake, but your mother's, too."

His tone changed with that last sentence, sounding the same as when he'd told her about that night in the safe house twenty years ago. The night when Eloise had fled.

It had been the middle of the night and as a baby, Kristin had cried out, awakening Jackson. When her complaints went unanswered, he rose, and found her alone in her crib, a note shoved onto the mobile dangling high above her. He scooped her into his arms, and she stopped crying. When he read the note, the one he eventually gave to her adoptive parents, the one Kristin found in her father's safe after her parents died, Jackson knew Eloise believed her life was no longer safe. She'd left because the Mob had found her, even at that safe house—

"Kristin?"

She started, coming back to the moment. "Yes?"

"Don't tell anyone about this conversation, and say nothing about your mother. We'll find her, rest assured of that, but we don't want you to lead the Martino family to her first. You'll both end up dead."

Kristin wet her lips. Dead? She swallowed. "I—I'll be very careful."

She disconnected, and with a shaky sigh, set her phone down on the table. Not find her mother? Give up her search? That was easy for Jackson McGraw to say. He wasn't dealing with the loss she had right now. He didn't hurt inside the way she hurt.

She should call Jackson back and tell him he had no right to order her not to find her mother.

Toying with her small phone, she squared her shoulders and flipped it open.

Then, she jumped.

That tall man who had strode in a few moments ago, the one she'd believed to be the P.I. she'd hired, now towered over her tiny table. She ran her gaze up his tall length, until she found piercing blue eyes drilling into her.

"Kristin Perry, I assume?"

Zane Black knew Kristin immediately. On Friday, she'd called him, her soft, lilting voice giving him a clear impression of what she looked like, clearer than he'd ever had before with a client. Some people looked the opposite of how they sounded, but not Kristin Perry.

Wide, green eyes blinked at him. Eyes soaked in fear, he thought. Around them, the bustle of the café softened as if waiting for her answer. But all she did was flip closed her phone and set it back on the table, with a slight shake.

"You *are* Kristin Perry, aren't you?" he asked. Even to his own ears, he sounded gruff.

She nodded jerkily, as if gathering wild thoughts together. Finally, with one more blink and a swallow, she spoke. "Yes. And you are…?"

"Zane Black." She knew who he was, surely? She'd asked him to meet her here. She'd noticed his arrival.

Something was off and he didn't like it when his suspicions were roused. That usually meant trouble was coming.

No, this wasn't quite the woman he'd spoken to on the

phone, the calm, quiet woman who sounded shy, but determined. This woman was scared, confused. "May I join you?" he asked.

"Yes, of course. Please, sit down." When he did, she glanced around and then leaned forward. "Um, call me Kristin. Ms. Perry sounds so formal."

Zane had made it his job to read body language and could quite accurately guess what people were thinking.

And this pretty young woman was already regretting her decision to ask him to come.

Zane sat back, wondering if he would get the brush-off. When the waiter appeared, he ordered an iced tea. Unsweetened. Then he turned his attention to her. "You mentioned on the phone you're trying to locate a woman. Do you have her name?"

Kristin bit her lip. Zane watched the motion intently, finding the little habit oddly attractive.

"I have very little information, I'm afraid. I know what the woman's name was years ago, and her approximate age, but that's pretty much it. I know she was living in Montana about twenty-one years ago."

"Is she a relative?"

Again, she bit her lip. "I'd rather not say at this point. I need you to be very discreet."

"I'm always discreet."

"No." She leaned forward, her voice dropping as her expression steeled. "I need you to find this woman without *anyone* ever knowing you're looking for her."

He lifted his eyebrows. "I can do that, too."

She paused, as if wanting to add more, but not convinced that she should. Impatient, he pulled out his notepad and pen, and set it on the table between them to write. His iced tea arrived and he shoved the cold glass to one side.

"No!"

He looked up, meeting her wide, green eyes and noting the straight brown hair that threatened to fall into them. Her look could easily be interpreted as benign, innocent, had he not just seen a cool determination behind it. "No, what?" he asked.

"I don't want you to take notes. I need you to remember everything I say. I can't risk your notebook being stolen."

His pen hovered over his pad, irritation tempting him to write anyway. But when her eyes filled with pleading, Zane's hand froze.

He battled his capitulation. He didn't like giving in. "You want me to remember everything you say to me? Don't you think that's a bit unreasonable? I can assure you that no one gets my notebook, Kristin. No one."

"Just humor me, okay? For a little while?" Her voice developed a velvet tone to it. With her wide, innocent eyes and perfect cream complexion, this young woman could probably get whatever she wanted from any man in town.

Yet, if he was reading her right, he bet she'd never asked a soul for anything, never manipulated a man before. Until now. He was tempted to test her determination, to see if there really was silk over steel where her will was concerned.

But a battle of wills was pointless and he had no taste for such foolishness. He'd had his fill of that nonsense years ago.

And besides, he found himself not wanting to argue with the beautiful Kristin Perry.

Slowly, he put away his pad and pen.

"Thank you."

Zane barely heard the words over the other conversations around them. But the gratitude rang clearly. "So, tell me about the woman you want me to find."

"She's around forty years old, has brown hair and green eyes, slim-boned and with a scar on her right cheek near her lips. It's in the shape of a rose petal."

He watched her hand drift up to her temple to smooth her hair. As if noticing his keen interest, she dropped her arm immediately.

"A rose petal?" he echoed. What on earth was the shape of a rose petal?

"Yes, you know. Rounded, with a slight point at one end."

"Okay," he began. "What's this woman's name?"

"Eloise."

"What's her relationship to you?"

A pause. "Like I said before, I can't say. I mean, I don't think it's something we need to discuss."

Zane pulled in a deep breath, then eased it out slowly to smooth over his growing impatience. Was this woman using him? Had he pegged her wrong when he'd thought she'd never manipulated men before?

This was fast becoming a big waste of time. He didn't need any more evasive people in his life, not after dealing that last time with his own parents. "Look, Kristin, I can't find a person with such vague information."

"What I've told you isn't vague, Mr. Black."

"Call me Zane."

"Fine. I told you her name, as I know it, and a basic description. She's somewhere in Montana."

"Which is a big state. How do you know she's here?"

"An acquaintance told me."

The person she'd spoken to a moment ago, the one who'd seemed to have dropped a bombshell? "And this person couldn't tell you anything more than that?"

"No."

"Have you begun to search for her by yourself?"

Color seeped into her cheeks, and her neck turned an attractive pink. "I asked around a few places."

He leaned forward, trying a stern look to stem the pull of her perfect features. Pretty girls were a dime a dozen in a college town, more so in this small town of Westbrook, he thought. He refused to be lured by her innocent eyes and classic good looks. "Kristin, you need to be more forthcoming here. I don't want to waste your money by doing things you've already done. So tell me. Where have you been?"

"I thought she'd gone south, to a bigger urban area like Missoula, so I went down there. But I could only go for the day. I've, um, been busy lately."

Busy doing what? he wondered. "More than half the state of Montana is south of Missoula. You need to be specific about where you think she went."

"I can't be. I asked at the city hall in Missoula and the public records, and at the tech colleges and such, in case she'd taken some courses. But I found nothing."

"Why those places?"

She shrugged. "I had to start somewhere. Getting an education is important. But I realized that I needed help. I'd lost a bit of my schooling this past spring because of personal issues, and I need to make it up this summer. The university offers summer courses. I can't spend my time doing both things."

Still a bit evasive, she was. He made a mental note to find out what kind of personal issues she'd dealt with this past spring. "Any other places?"

She paused, pursed her lips and then wet them. After swallowing, she answered him. "I found out that Eloise lived for a while at a foster home in Chicago. I talked to the woman who ran it. She's supposed to, er, send me some info."

She didn't want to tell him, that, he noticed. Why? Was the idea of a foster home difficult? Or had the woman asked for anonymity? Surely she would know that she shouldn't be offering information about the children in her care, even the ones who had probably aged out long ago.

Abruptly, Kristin leaned forward. "Please, Zane, I need your help. A friend recommended you, and I *really* need to find this woman. But it has to be done very discreetly."

If his gut was telling him correctly, the woman was her mother.

A mom. Supposedly the one person in a child's life who should love unconditionally. Yeah, like that happened.

Still, didn't he already love unconditionally the brother he'd come to Westbrook to find? Without even knowing him?

He did. Zane noticed Kristin's hand slip from her lap up onto the table between them, to rest there like a shy, stray animal in search of food or affection.

Did he really need this case? No, not for the money. He was sensible enough to have saved so that he could spend his summer searching exclusively for his lost brother, though he had yet to start. He didn't need to follow weak clues from an evasive woman. He'd only agreed to meet her because he'd been intrigued by that smooth, velvet voice.

He stood. "I'm sorry, Kristin, but I'm going to need more than just the few things you've told me. If you're not willing to say more, then you can't expect anyone to find your mom."

She gasped. "How did you know she was my mother?"

"I'm good at my job. I know how to read people." He'd learned that the hard way, the way any battered kid learns to watch a parent for those subtle signs that a beating was imminent. "I see."

He watched as her eyes welled up. *Great.* Feeling he was being a bit too hard on her, he planted his hands on the table, one on each side of hers. Her body tensed as she eased her hand closer to her body.

"Kristin, you need to trust the person you hire to find her, and obviously you're not ready to do that. When you are, call me back."

"It's not a matter of trust here."

"Then you're being too stubborn for some reason. I need cooperation and trust before I can go any further with this."

"But I need to find her. It's a matter of—" She cut off her words.

"Of life and death?" He threw her a dubious look. "Then go to the police."

"I can't. And I can't explain why."

"Then *I* can't help you." He straightened. The café around him came into sharp focus. Being a typical college-town café, it had atmosphere aplenty, right down to the poster styled mirror mounted on the wall behind Kristin. In that brief instance, he caught his reflection.

Did his brother look like him? For the past two years, since his mother had finally told him the truth, he'd searched for the man, a full brother two years younger. Would he ever meet him?

He looked down at Kristin. "You've got my number. Call when you're ready." His heel drilled into the battered pine floor as he pivoted. He could feel her gaze glued to his back as he walked out the door.

The sun had already warmed the day, more than expected, he thought. He'd been in northwest Montana for two years and had noticed that springtime here could mean anything weather-wise.

Today, the sun beat down on him and he pulled from his jacket pocket a pair of sunglasses. He strode across the street, noticing the traffic had increased with a small town's version of morning rush hour.

"Zane!"

He turned. Kristin stood in the café's entrance, holding the door with one hand, her purse with the other. Once she'd caught his attention, she released the handle and trotted across the sidewalk, cutting through the increasing flow of pedestrians. The favorable weather was luring people outside in droves. Older people and students who'd chosen to stay the summer to get extra credits, a popular thing to do here, all seemed to be walking to work or school today.

For the first time, he could fully see what she was wearing. Dark jeans, a thin university hoodie and, over it, a light vest. Typical college-student wear around here.

She's changed her mind, he thought, having decided that vagueness wasn't going to locate her mother. Smart girl, but frankly, he wasn't interested. His own family, his mom especially, had been secretive enough. Sure, she had her own trouble with his father, but she hadn't once stood up for her adopted son, the boy she'd promised to care for. Instead, she'd kept secrets from him, even lying to save her own skin sometimes. Leaving his skin to be blistered from beatings.

He'd had a lifetime's worth of secretive garbage, and he didn't feel like dragging the same stuff from another reluctant woman.

At the outer edge of his vision, a truck accelerated, grinding first gear into second as it approached. Kristin stopped between the cars parked on an angle, her glance down the busy street telling Zane she also saw the truck coming. He waited. *Should he take her on as a client?*

Depends on what she says, he decided.

He glanced again at the midsize delivery truck, old and battered, with a grizzled, bearded driver. As the power train jerked into third gear, the vehicle lurched closer.

A scream sliced through the air, and Zane snapped his head back over.

Her arms flaying out wildly, Kristin was falling directly into the truck's path.

TWO

Zane leaped forward, only to be blocked by the truck. The driver laid on the horn, adding to the sound of screeching brakes as the huge vehicle careened to a lumbering stop.

Zane slammed into its left side and after he spun once, he raced around the back.

Kristin was sprawled facedown by the right front tire, her purse beside her. Zane sliced through the growing crowd as she began to roll over.

"Don't move," he told her. "Stay still for a minute. You may be hurt."

The truck driver hurried around the front bumper. "Is she all right? I didn't see her until she jumped out at me!"

Kristin sat up. "I didn't jump. I was pushed."

The driver stepped back in shock. Zane took the opportunity to move in front of him. As he did, Kristin threw back her hair. "Someone shoved me!"

Immediately, Zane glanced around, stretching his vision from one end of the street to the other. Apart from the crowd that had gathered, he saw no one hurrying away. Murmurs threaded through the onlookers at her accusation, each person checking out their neighbor. He watched each surprised face. No one looked guilty.

Zane stooped to take her arm. "I told you not to move."

She grabbed him and pulled herself to her feet. "I'm fine. A little scraped up, that's all." Then, with a shocked gaze, she looked around. "Didn't you see him? The man who pushed me?"

The driver shook his head. "I laid on the horn when I first saw you," he cried out. "It looked like you'd stumbled!"

She threw off Zane's helping hand. "I didn't stumble. I was pushed. I distinctly felt two hands on my back." She looked at Zane. "You didn't see him, either?"

"No." Inwardly, he cringed at his short word. It wasn't as though he suspected her of lying, but with the blank looks from the crowd gathering around them, he wondered briefly if she'd staged this to get his attention.

Was this a ploy to avoid telling her precious secret, all the while gaining sympathy and an agreement to take her case?

Zane gritted his teeth. His mother had done something similar when he'd begun to ask questions. She'd faked an illness to avoid the truth.

Kristin straightened. "Well, someone pushed me." With a hand that was definitely shaking, she smoothed her straight brown hair. For one brief moment, he caught sight of a long white scar just above her temple. Then, as quickly as it was exposed, it slipped back into hiding beneath the straight cloak of shiny brown tresses.

And as if realizing she was creating a scene, Kristin grabbed her purse and brushed off her jeans. "I know what I felt. I *was* pushed, but managed to roll away from the truck in the nick of time."

Zane moved her away from the crowd. It wasn't such a good idea to attract this much attention. Kristin had been evasive for a reason, and while he hated secrecy, he knew she shouldn't be standing in the middle of the street if she needed some privacy or protection. And as a private investigator, he preferred to keep a low profile, as well. Playing hero for all to see wasn't what his profession was about. He was trained to blend into the crowd, notice things without being noticed.

To that end, he steered her around the truck and toward his car, to get away from local curiosity.

"Let's go."

"Where?"

"To the truck stop out by the highway. We'll talk there."

She followed him to his car, hesitantly, stopping short of climbing in. "I don't get into strangers' cars."

"Good advice for anyone." Then, pulling out his car keys, he handed them to her. "You can drive if it makes you feel safer. Do you know the truck stop I'm talking about?"

"Of course. I was bor— I mean I grew up here."

He caught her correction, but decided to ignore it for now.

"But driving your car isn't going to make it safer for me," she reasoned.

"Let me show you my ID. But frankly, you should have asked for it as soon as I sat down in the café."

"You're the first private investigator I've ever hired. And you come highly recommended." After checking out his ID, she took the keys and clicked the unlock button before tossing her purse into the back. With a short hesitation, she climbed in behind the wheel. Automatically, she moved the seat up to accommodate her shorter stature.

She started the car. "Does this mean you'll take my case?"

"Maybe. Who recommended me?"

"Jake Downs. His sister and I are in the same chemistry class. He's the locksmith who helped me open my father's safe a few months ago. We made a mess of the wall at home because Jake had to take the safe to his shop and drill through the side of it just to open it. You know, look at the lock from the inside? When I asked if he knew any private investigators, he recommended you." She shrugged. "And he also recommended a good drywaller to fix the wall in my father's office."

Zane knew Jake Downs. A good locksmith, accredited and bonded, with a cocky charm that seemed in total contradiction with the man's strong personal faith. He was a Christian, and had even invited him to church once.

Zane had declined. For work reasons, he'd said. Truth was, the cost of believing was just a bit too high for him.

Still, he nodded. "I know Jake, but I didn't know he had a sister."

"Maggie. She's the funniest person ever, so we don't get much chem work done." She paused a few seconds as she pulled into traffic. "She works at the lab at the university."

She glanced at him as she signaled to merge onto the highway. It took her a moment to ask, "Have you decided to take my case?"

He paused. "Have you decided to trust me?"

By now, they'd reached the truck stop, it being only a short drive down the highway. After parking, she turned to him. "Zane, I need to find my biological mother. I don't know much about her, but I know she's in danger."

Hmm. Was this her idea of trust? A few mysterious words? "In danger of what?"

"Of being murdered."

The words hung between them in the car, as Zane

watched Kristin's eyes grow wide with some instant re-alization and she sucked in a sharp breath.

"What's wrong?" he asked. "Besides the obvious fact you think your biological mother is in danger."

Her expression turned hollow as she stared out the windshield. "They're after me," she whispered. "Jackson was right!" She bit her lip before adding, "I should never have gone to that guy's trial! But that couldn't have been how…"

What on earth was she talking about? "Look at me, Kristin. What's going on?"

She turned toward him, her eyes like a Japanese cartoon. "I went to Vincent Martino's trial," she breathed out. "That must have been where they saw me, but he didn't say it was."

He shook his head and frowned. "Whose trial?" He itched to reach for his notebook, but stopped himself, instead committing the name to memory. "Did you have to testify?"

"No. It's a long story."

"Where was it?"

"Chicago." She blinked. "While I was there, I met up with Jackson McGraw again. He's an FBI agent there. I'd met him some months ago when I started the search for my mother. During a recess at the trial—"

"Wait!" he interrupted. "Are you talking about the mobster Vincent Martino? Wasn't he convicted, but es-caped custody?" He stared intently at her. "What was so important about going to his trial? That courtroom was probably the most dangerous place to be in all of the country."

"It was also said to be the safest place in the country."

Zane sat back, trying to recall the details that had

flooded the news last month. With the tightest security since the president was sworn in, the judge would only allow those closely associated with the trial to be in the courtroom. How did this woman get in?

More to the point, why did she think Vincent Martino was now after her? What was going on?

"Drive. Start the engine and drive," he told her.

"Where are we going?"

"To the police station. You need to report what happened to you."

She opened her mouth to argue, but shut it again.

"Is there a problem?" he asked.

"I should make a phone call first. It won't take long." She twisted around for her purse.

"And in the meantime your assailant's trail goes cold. The police can help you, but you can't be calling a girlfriend first."

Their gazes locked. He could easily see the irritated indecision in hers. "The police can only help you if you're timely, Kristin."

"It wasn't to call a girlfriend." She looked exasperated. "It's a long story."

He'd hurt her feelings, he noted. Still, she needed to see the police. "The police should know about it, Kristin."

Finally, she nodded. After starting the engine, she carefully eased from her parking spot and out onto the highway.

He wanted to ask her a thousand questions, mostly sparked by his own curiosity, but common sense told him to report the incident in front of the café.

And then walk away.

Yes, Zane. Walk far away. You don't need this hassle.

And yet, he argued silently with himself, there was

something earnest about her, a deep hurting quality that tugged at his protective instincts.

The police station came into view, an ordinary brick-and-mortar building on the other side of the town. But after parking in the visitor spot, Kristin made no effort to climb out. Zane sat there patiently, staring out at the line of snow-topped mountains that trimmed the horizon behind the station. In front of them, the flag jerked about in the increasing wind.

"You have to report what happened to you, Kristin."

"I don't know. Jackson said—"

This Jackson guy must have a title in the FBI, but he'd find that out later. "Never mind what he said. You think someone tried to kill you, so you need to talk to the police. If it has anything to do with the Martino family, you need to let them know even more."

She snapped her head over. "How do you know what I need? Or what I think, or anything?"

"You have the face of an angel, Kristin. Every thought that runs through your head is displayed loud and clear to those who know how to read people. And I've made it my business to read people. *You* think what's happened to you is related to the Martino family. And we both know you're not telling me everything, but you will tell the police."

"Maybe."

"No maybes about it. You obviously don't trust me, but surely, you'll trust the local police force."

She sat ramrod still, not answering him for a few minutes. He had the time to wait her out, but when he looked up at her face, a tear rolled down her perfectly clear cheek. It dropped to her jeans.

He groaned inwardly. "What's wrong?"

She hastily brushed the tear away. "The last time I was

here was to pick up my adoptive parents' things. The police had come to my door and taken me to the hospital." She looked at him with hollow eyes. "Did you know that they have a morgue in the basement there? I had to identify my mother and father. They'd been in a car crash south of here. The police were actually willing to take me to where they died, but I… It was the worst thing to ever happen to me. I couldn't do it."

She swallowed, obviously fighting back difficult emotions. "Then a policewoman took me home and spent the night with me, until one of the ladies from the church could come and stay. A couple of days later, I was asked to come here to collect my parents' things. They handed me a box and two bags of stuff that was broken and splattered with—" She inhaled shakily. "Then the police were done with me. I haven't been back since."

Zane slumped. He remembered a crash about five months ago. The roads were clear, but still the car had plunged over a short embankment into Lindbergh Lake. Both the husband and wife had died. The autopsies and even tearing apart the car couldn't reveal any reason for the accident. The story fell off the radar shortly after their funeral.

They were her parents?

Abruptly, Kristin threw open the door and climbed out.

"Kristin!" Zane scrambled out. "I had no idea. You should have said something."

She colored as she pulled her short vest closer around her neck. Outside the center of town, the wind was stronger and cooler. "I should be able to come to the police station without tears, right? I'm a big girl. Regardless of Jackson's warning, I need to report what happened to me. I mean, he'd insist I tell the police if he knew I'd been pushed into traffic, right? They'd be able to investigate it better than he could."

She straightened her shoulders, obviously trying to look taller than she really was. As a petite, slender woman, she couldn't really pull it off.

Why wouldn't this Jackson guy trust the police? Why even say that? Zane thought. Unless it had something to do with that phone call she'd received back in the café. The one he now figured came from Jackson.

He was from the FBI, Kristin had said. He wouldn't fool around with her life.

Several government cars pulled into the parking lot. Kristin moved to one side to allow them to park. The wind raised a few strands of her hair, flicking them over to one side. His hand itched to set them back in place and cover that scar she hid so well. "You don't have to go in there."

"I should. I should remember what my pastor told me. My parents are together with Jesus now. And the Lord wouldn't give me any situation I can't handle. I handled their deaths." She looked over at the station, as if steeling herself. "I can do this."

Zane shifted uncomfortably. Another one like Jake Downs that believed God is good, even when He dumped on you. That was because they didn't have the childhood Zane had.

"Nonetheless, you don't have to go in."

She wavered a bit, he could see. Then she shook her head. "I should. Someone pushed me in front of that truck and I wouldn't be here right now if I hadn't managed to roll away quickly. God was looking out for me."

"If God was looking out for you, He wouldn't have put that truck on the road or that idiot on the sidewalk."

"He gave me the agility I needed." A frown marked her

forehead. "This isn't the time to debate the merits of my faith. I need to go into this station sooner or later. I'm going in, now." She lifted her chin. "And maybe I can show you that I'm sincere in doing this, so that you'll help me find my biological mother."

He hated her intuition, not to mention the guilt she was dumping on him. But before he could say anything, she added with a soft, sweet smile, "I appreciate all you've done so far."

"I haven't done anything," he growled.

"You were there for me at the café."

He took her arm and steered her toward the front door. He hadn't done a single thing for her yet, nor had he promised to do anything. And yet she was thanking him.

He should help her.

But still, a voice within him whispered, *she hasn't told you much. All you've heard is a sad, little story.*

He glanced down at her as she tugged free of his grip and moved forward. He watched her straighten up and stiffen her spine.

Across the back of her vest were two faint smears of something dark and iridescent. Some kind of grease? From the hands of the man who pushed her?

Before he could say anything, she strode toward the front door. With a frown, he took the few long steps needed to catch up with her.

Inside the station, a police officer recognized Kristin, and led them down to a small office. She hesitated in the doorway before pushing inside. They sat down and Kristin began to speak.

She told her story, haltingly, he thought.

And leaving out, he noticed, the part of why she had asked to meet Zane.

And the part about Martino's trial. Zane kept his mouth

shut, deciding he would say something only if it became necessary. Maybe she was rethinking that just because she'd attended a trial did not necessarily mean the convicted felon would go after her.

The officer recorded it all, getting the statement written up quickly for her to sign.

"You should take her vest," Zane suggested to the man when all was done.

The officer frowned. "Why?"

Zane answered by asking Kristin to remove the vest. With a small frown, she peeled it off, and Zane spread it out on the table between him and the officer. The dark smudges he'd seen earlier stood out starkly in the cool fluorescent lights. They shimmered like some kind of special automotive grease. The two marks were shaped like fingerprints.

"Whoever pushed her left those marks. They may reveal fingerprints."

The officer retrieved a large paper bag and set the vest in it, then wrote out a receipt for her. "I'll have a look at it later, but you must remember that this is a college town, and students do stupid things, even early in the morning. Someone could have just jostled you, Ms. Perry, and then slipped back into the crowd so he wouldn't be accused of anything."

"I distinctly felt two hands on my back."

"This is a thick vest. Are you sure?"

"Absolutely." She stiffened her shoulders. "Why would I lie?"

The officer shook his head. "I'm not saying you're lying. You may be mistaken. We often get reports of students jumping the gun on things that later prove to be just an accident, or not real at all."

She glared. "I know what I felt."

"You just lost both parents, Ms. Perry," the officer continued calmly. "It can have a devastating effect on people."

Zane's hand shot out to stop Kristin before she did or said something stupid. He could feel her muscles tighten under his fingers. "Can you just check the vest?"

"Sure." The officer looked doubtful, but then shrugged. "We'll see what we can find, but don't expect too much."

"I understand." Rising, she shoved out her hand. "Thank you. I hope you can find something useful on that vest. And I hope you find who did this to me."

"You said no one saw anything. It may be hard to do."

"Surely if you ask around, someone will remember something. People aren't going to accuse others right in public, but they may be willing to talk in private." Kristin looked hopefully at the man.

The officer shrugged before shaking her hand and then Zane's. They left the office, passing several plainclothes officers who watched Kristin closely. Was she known to them because of her adoptive parents' untimely deaths? Minutes later, she and Zane were outside again.

She sighed. "That felt like a waste of my time."

Zane stopped her as she walked toward his car. "Why didn't you say anything about the trial?"

"Because of the way Jackson was talking. Like I shouldn't trust anyone. Plus, it may not have been related."

"You thought it was a few minutes ago."

"I know." She looked uncertain. "I had second thoughts. I wanted to go in there. I wanted to tell him, but I thought of my parents, and Jackson, and even my mother, then when that officer first looked at me, remembering me from the crash, I just lost all…strength. I'm sorry."

"It's okay. You've been through some rough times."

She blinked. "Have you ever lost someone you love?"

He thought of his parents, and the beatings, the way his mother wouldn't look at him for days on end. When he was young, he thought she was mad at him. Later, he realized she was saving her own skin. He didn't miss them when they died, and he hated that truth.

"I need to call Jackson back before I say anything more to the police," she said when he didn't answer her.

"How do you know you can trust him?"

"He works for the FBI. I was even in his office, and that building is like a fortress." She paused, tossing her hand out. "Okay, I trust him, that's all. He seems to be very careful dealing with me. It's almost as though he treats me like a princess or something really delicate." Her hands flew up in defense. "I know that sounds egotistical, but it's not. I think he genuinely wants what's best for me, and is determined to find my mother. But he's afraid my mother and I will both be killed."

Pausing, she shook her head. "I don't even know if I'm remembering his words correctly. I'll call him back to make sure. He sounded as though he thought Vincent Martino was planning to come after me. That guy might already know where I am because of the trial." She started walking again. "I realize that I'm not making any sense, but it's hard to explain."

Zane stopped them. Holding out his hand, he said, "Give me the car keys. I need to do something."

Kristin handed him his keys. "Like what?"

He looked at her. She stopped halfway to the car, holding herself close and rubbing her arms. The cold wind, now coming down from Canada, defiantly tossed around her hair. The flag nearby fluttered even more noisily. "I have to get you home so you can get a coat to wear. You do own a decent jacket, don't you?"

"Of course I do. But the vest was cute and I wasn't cold this morning. And I certainly didn't expect to surrender it to the police today."

Zane peeled off his sheepskin jacket and handed it to her. She was about to decline it, he could tell, but caught his stern look and changed her mind.

"Now you'll get cold," she said as she slipped into it. The ends of the sleeves dangled beyond her fingers until she hugged herself.

"I'll be okay. This won't take long. I'm going to collect my own forensic samples."

"But you already made me surrender my vest."

"You leaned back onto my car seat," he answered. "There should be some residue there."

"Can you do that?"

"I'm trained to collect evidence and have it still be legally admissible in court." He unlocked the doors and dug a small kit from the backseat. He then took a photograph of the mess she'd smeared on the back of the driver's seat. Once he examined it again, he lifted the smear and then swabbed what was left.

Over his shoulder, Kristin peered at his handiwork. "Do you think you'll find fingerprints in that?"

Zane shook his head. "They probably didn't transfer, especially considering how much it's smeared. But I might find some trace DNA."

"Do you have your own lab? How long will it take?"

He laughed, and then straightened out of the car. "I'm guessing you watch too many crime shows on TV."

She reddened. "I'm a full-time student trying to major in business and minor in science. I don't have time to watch much TV."

"Sorry," he answered her berate. "Anyway, to answer

your question, no, I don't have my own lab. I'll use that independent lab you mentioned before."

"Good. I've never been in it. I wasn't a chem minor until this past year. I did art history until I realized that I couldn't tell a Vermeer from a Van Gogh, even if the artists were telling me which was which. But with Maggie working there, we may be able to get it done quickly."

"Excellent. We'll go over just as soon as you pick up your jacket. Try to get a warmer one than your vest."

She glanced up at the sky. "The day was supposed to be warm."

"I've only been here two years, but I've already noticed how unpredictable spring can be."

"You've only been here two years? Why did you come here?"

He packed away his collection kit and draped a car blanket over the driver's seat before answering. "I came here to find my brother. I was adopted and when I learned I had a full brother who might be in Montana, I decided to move here and look for him. I just didn't think I'd still be looking for him two years later."

She looked crestfallen. "Two years! I was hoping to find my mother within a few weeks."

"I hope you do, too." He felt the urge to draw her into his arms, but checked it quickly. He hadn't even decided to accept her case yet, so getting mixed up with her too much would not only be a waste of time, but highly unprofessional, as well. "Let's get your jacket."

With Kristin directing him, Zane drove to her house. The small, well-kept bungalow was slightly outside of town on a quiet street that intersected a tertiary highway.

Zane glanced around. There was no other traffic at the

moment, he saw. But for a place this quiet, the feeling of being watched lingered heavily on him.

Way too heavily.

THREE

Zane watched Kristin slip into the modest bungalow, only to exit a few seconds later with a faux suede tailored jacket in a dark blue color. She'd also chosen a long, thin scarf to ward off the cool breeze. She'd wrapped it once around her neck.

He let out a long breath as he shook his head. She obviously did not know how to protect herself. If someone wanted to harm her, a long scarf would be a perfect weapon.

She'd been pushed into traffic; he believed that, not only because of the smudges, but also because to trip right at that moment was simply too coincidental.

And he didn't believe in coincidences. Nor did he believe in wearing things that an attacker could use against a person.

Patience, he told himself. *She's not as cynical as you are. She probably hadn't seen her father try to strangle her mother.*

"I've got to teach you how to dress," he muttered as she climbed in his car again.

"I beg your pardon!"

He had to smile at her shocked but polite words. She

had excellent diction, though her accent was definitely northwestern. "I mean that you need to choose clothes that can't be used as weapons."

She looked down at herself. "Like what?"

"Your scarf. If someone is after you, then you must not give them anything they can use against you." He paused, then added, "And you need to not act so…" He fought for the right words, then knowing they'd never come, he said, "regally."

She tightened her jaw. "I'm not a princess." She eased off on the outraged expression, looking more hurt than anything else. "My adoptive mother, Anna, was an English teacher, born of British parents. My father was a lawyer here in town and, before that, in Billings. He was good at his job. Projecting an air of confidence was important to him."

"Your mother was a teacher?"

Looking sad, she said, "Well, yes, until I was—came along. She retired to stay home with me. She loved being a mother."

He softened. He knew he'd hurt her, but she needed to hear what he'd said for her own safety. And suddenly, her safety meant a lot to him. "I didn't mean to offend you. I don't want you hurt, that's all."

Kristin seemed to be considering his warning. "I'll try to do better. And you're right. When I first started at the university, I attended a seminar on campus safety. I think they did mention scarves and long ponytails being things that an attacker could grab. I'm sorry. I just didn't figure I would ever be a target for someone."

"Which means we need to figure out why, not to mention how you've become a target." He threw her a sidelong glance.

"Of course." She looked uncomfortable as she peeled off the scarf, pausing a moment as if she wanted to say more. "So, are we going to take your samples to the lab?"

"Yes. I want to catch them before they close for lunch." He started his car, and within minutes, they had returned to the center of Westbrook. He knew the lab, having used it a few times since he moved here. And maybe with Kristin's connections, they'd get some answers quickly.

Because he had a nagging feeling that they'd need those answers soon.

As they entered the lab, Maggie, Kristin's chem partner approached with a broad smile and Kristin found herself answering with her own smile. Zane briefly told Maggie what he needed to have done. She nodded as he passed her the sample he'd taken from his car.

Maggie studied the smear Zane handed her. "I don't think you'll get any fingerprints, but we'll see what this stuff is. I can test it for human DNA, too, but it'll have to go out to the lab in Helena for a full analysis. That could take three weeks or more, depending on how much you're willing to pay." She brightened. "In the meantime, we should have the results on what this is in a couple of days."

"That's fine." Once the paperwork was completed, Zane turned toward the door.

Immediately, Maggie flashed a brilliant smile and a thumbs-up for approval. Kristin felt herself blanch. Was Maggie thinking that Zane was a boyfriend and she was merely following him around today for lack of anything better to do?

Zane turned back and peered at Maggie, who dropped the smile like the cheeky girl she was. With a frown, he said goodbye and held the door for Kristin.

Outside, Kristin trotted down the short flight of stone steps toward the parking lot, glad to be away from the embarrassing situation in the lab. Zane, a boyfriend? Sure, he was handsome, with some kind of indefinable strength, but still…

But still what? Suddenly, she felt as if she had no argument against Zane. Quite the opposite, really.

Kristin felt herself redden further. The brick buildings around them had cut the wind considerably, and she was glad she didn't have to smooth her hair constantly in order to hide her scar. She didn't need to add that to her embarrassment.

At the bottom step, her scalp near her scar tingling, Kristin stopped, remembering words from the note her birth mother had written Jackson.

Kristin almost died because of the path I've needed to take.

Years ago, her adoptive parents had told her that the scar was something she'd been born with. And to forget about it.

Like a dutiful daughter, she'd dropped the questions. She had her answer, now, from Jackson, and it was as shocking as finding out she'd been adopted out of state, not born here as her other birth certificate claimed.

She *really* had come close to dying and today the truth was sinking in even more deeply.

But it being a frightful souvenir and not a birth defect she'd always tried to hide still didn't make her want it exposed, and certainly not to Zane. He was altogether too perceptive and with all that had happened, she felt exposed enough.

Zane took her arm and hurried her to his car. "That's all we can do for now."

She set aside her turbulent thoughts. "Does this mean you'll take my case?" Honestly, she was beginning to hate that mantra, but couldn't help ask again.

He paused. "I've been considering taking the summer off, but—" A short ring rippled through the air. Zane pulled out his cell phone and flipped it open. "Just a second. It's a text from a friend."

Stepping away from her, he stared at the small screen. His mouth fell open and his shoulders drooped. As she watched, the air around them felt as if it dropped in temperature.

Bad news.

Punching out numbers, Zane stepped farther from Kristen. She folded her arms against the sudden chill, staring at his back as he listened intently to the person on the other end. When he finally hung up, he turned. His jaw looked tight enough to snap.

Oh, yes, something was definitely wrong. She hurried over to him. "What's the matter?"

"Nothing. Let's go. I'd like to talk to the waiter at the café again."

She struggled to keep up with his long stride. "Something's wrong, isn't it? Is it about me?"

"No, it's not about you at all." He unlocked his car and held the door open for her. "Just get in."

Biting her lip, she obeyed. When Zane sat down behind the wheel, she touched his arm. "If it's not about me, then, is there anything I can do?"

"No. Just a lead in another case I'd been following. It's a dead end, that's all."

"I'm sorry. Is it about your brother? Maybe I can help you. I've lived here all my life. Well, almost all my life, so I know a lot of people. My father had a thriving law practice here, and Mom knew everyone."

His eyes widened. Though the bad news had marred the blue of his eyes like soft cirrus clouds wash out a clear sky, she could see shock easily in them. "You're not going to dig into your father's private files, are you?"

She shook her head. "Oh, no! His files went to his law partner. I'd never do that! I was just thinking if you were looking for someone, maybe I could help. Do you think he was a local?"

"I'd been hoping he was local. But I was wrong."

"Who? I might know the name."

Zane's mouth thinned. "I only know his last name is Kendall." He spelled it.

She sat back in the seat and shook her head. "Kendall. Hmm. I'm not sure. How old is he?"

"Two years younger than me."

She stopped in mid-thought. His brother. Zane had moved here to find him, and now that one lead has dissolved. What was next for him? Would he move on?

She watched Zane's clean profile, his straight nose and strong chin. His dark hair fell into his eyes slightly, and his brooding good looks and casual clothes seemed to fit well on the campus around them. The hurt in his expression, however, did not.

Suddenly, she didn't want him to move out of the area to continue his search somewhere else. But she had to ask, "What's next in your search?"

He slid his gaze sideways across the car's front seats to her. "I don't know. That guy on the phone was following my strongest lead, but it didn't pan out."

Her heart swelled in sympathy. They were both searching. In a way, she'd found a kindred spirit. "I'm sorry."

"It's all right. I've built a good business here, and searching for my brother is something I do when I have the time. I have even less information on him than you have on your mother so I always knew I may never find him."

"So you're back to square one now?"

"I have one much weaker lead out there, but am not expecting anything to come of it."

He watched her, as if, she wondered, he was also looking for understanding. Her heart lurched. He was hurting, too. He was struggling to find a connection with his past. And like her, he may never find his family.

"Let's get some lunch. My treat," she suggested to break the melancholy settling over them. "There's a new restaurant downtown that has great Mexican food. If you like, you can tell me what you know about your brother. I'm no expert, but maybe you just need a fresh eye?"

He frowned at her and she tried a small, hopeful smile. She didn't feel like smiling, and yet, sticking with Zane brought a strange measure of comfort that made smiling that much easier. Besides, after that push into traffic, she didn't feel like being alone.

"Why don't we talk about you instead, Kristin?" he answered. "My search for my brother can wait, but yours can't. No one wants to kill me for it, but you are definitely in danger because of your search."

"Do you really think it's related to my mother?"

"I don't believe in coincidences, and they're piling up here. Your mother is in hiding, and right after you attend a related trial, you're in danger, as well?"

"I don't know anything, so there's no reason to kill me."

"I'm not saying you do know anything, but someone could be mistaking you for your mother. Do you look like her?"

She bit her lip. "I don't know. I've only ever seen one photo of her and I don't have it. It's hard to see a resemblance to yourself, I think."

Of course, she knew of another photo on its way to her. Zane may be able to confirm a resemblance.

Zane glanced around the parking lot, before zeroing in on her. "You want me to take on your case, but it's obvious that you're holding some things back. And the look on your face after you received that phone call this morning told me you didn't know what to do. Were you warned about me?"

"No! Well, not exactly." Boy, he was good. He was able to read her like a book. Should she tell him anything? Jackson had warned her of a leak. Anyone, including Zane, could use what they'd learn from her to find her mother, or inform the Mob, she wagered. How could she know for sure that he wouldn't tell the Martino family?

But what could Zane learn from her? She didn't have anything but a name, an old address from a foster home her mother had lived in, where that other photo had been taken, and very little else. She doubted her mother would use her real name and she certainly wouldn't contact her old foster home again. Kristin only wanted the photo because it was of her mother and had been offered to her.

Zane tilted his head. "I can help you find your mother. So why won't you tell me anything?"

If she found her mother, she reasoned to herself, she could warn her about the Martinos, about what Jackson had said. They could hide together, taking that time to get to know each other again. It would be so wonderful, and everything she'd dreamed of since her friend Jake had opened her father's safe and she'd found the adoption papers.

She swallowed. "I've been told to be very careful."

"Because of the Martino family? Why did you go to the trial then?"

"I had to see the man whose father had caused my mother to hide. But no one recognized me. I lightened my hair, and wore tinted glasses. And due to the security, those allowed into the courtroom were escorted in and out through a side door, and protected from the public."

"But afterward, you came straight back here?"

"No." She shook her head, understanding what he meant. "Jackson McGraw advised against that. After the trial, I wanted to thank one of the witnesses for the prosecution. He took me to the FBI building in the city. I talked to her there."

"Who was she?"

"Olivia Jarrod. She was the star witness in that trial."

"What did she say?"

"To me? Not much. I just thanked her for doing her best to get rid of the Martino family. Then I told her that I'd been separated from my mother for about twenty-one years and she said she hoped I would find my mother someday. The conversation didn't last long. She didn't want to stick around, and I didn't, either."

"So then you came straight home?"

She shook her head. "Jackson and I decided that I should take a flight to Maine to spend some time with a college friend. So I did. We climbed Mount Katahdin. Then we toured the East Coast for a week. After that, I returned here."

Her tone changed as she drilled a stare into him. They were sitting in his car. Around them, the campus had gone quiet. "Please, Zane, I can't tell you much, because I don't know much."

Zane's look darkened, as if he disagreed with her. But thankfully, he said nothing. She continued, faster than before. "But I need to find my mother. Let's have some lunch. We'll talk there."

She hadn't really expected Zane to agree, but he did, asking for the name of the restaurant. A swell of accomplishment filled her. He was willing to talk to her, perhaps to engender trust, or perhaps because he needed to talk, maybe about his own fruitless search. She didn't care about the reason. Suddenly, being with him warmed her, gave her a sense of connection.

At the restaurant, they found a booth in the back and ordered the daily special of quesadillas. After scribbling out their order, the waitress plunked down a large bowl of nacho chips and salsa. Kristin dug in. Catching Zane's eye, she shrugged. "I'm hungry. And when I'm stressed, I eat. I'm not one to starve myself, I'm afraid."

"Don't apologize. I think it's normal." He grimaced. "You may be a bit naïve, but at least you're not the thin, high-strung sort."

She lifted her eyebrows, wondering who was like that in his life that brought such a derisive comment. "There's a compliment in there, I'm sure. I just can't see it right now."

She picked up another chip and munched on it. At least he was talking. The stress of the call he'd made seemed to be wearing him down, loosening the cool grit that held him tightly together.

"It *is* a compliment. And you're honest about it." He tightened his jaw. "Believe me, I appreciate honesty."

Why shouldn't he? She stemmed her curiosity by changing the subject. "My church loves to eat. We'll use any excuse for a potluck lunch. No thin, high-strung ladies there." She pointed a corn chip at him. "You should come. There'll be snacks after the service this week."

Her offer slipped out automatically. She'd asked many of her college friends to church. Some had come, most had declined. Sleeping in on Sundays was too important to them.

He looked away, his jaw tight. "Once upon a time, I believed in God and all that. But the price was too high. You have to be perfect, and that's not me. In fact, if I have to be as good as my father thought he was, I'd rather not be a Christian at all."

She stopped chewing. The bitterness in his words bounced around their booth. She'd never heard such cold condemnation. What would her parents say to this?

Suddenly, the ache of grief weighed down her heart. Her parents *would* have known the right answer. They were wonderfully compassionate. They'd taken her in twenty-one years ago, finding themselves with a small child after many years alone. It must have been hard for them to keep up with a busy little toddler.

But enough of that. What could *she* say to Zane? He seemed so disappointed with God. How could she take that away?

She couldn't. Nor was it any of her business, no matter how sad it made her feel. With a sip of water, she swallowed the corn chip and hastened to change the subject. "You said you have a brother. Where are your parents?"

"Dead. Both my birth parents and my adoptive ones. I was adopted shortly after I was born," he told her tersely.

"So what clues led you here?"

"While I was living in upstate New York, I did a data search for the last name Kendall." He spelled the name. "My adoptive mother only ever told me the last name and only after a good deal of pressure. She was afraid of my adoptive father."

His jaw had tightened again, she noticed.

As if catching her curiosity, he cleared his throat and

took a chip. "Anyway, I got a break once with some on-line photos from Westbrook University. So I decided to move here and set up my business."

He dipped a chip into the salsa. "The lead today turned out to be no good."

Their meals arrived and when the server left them, Kristin stared at her food.

She snapped her attention back him, remembering why the name sounded familiar. "What did this Kendall guy study?"

"Art, specializing in oils, I'm told. I don't even know if he is my brother. He's already left the area."

Kristin set down her glass of water. "There's a painting in one of the lecture rooms that's signed 'Bobby Kendall' with that same spelling. It could be his. It's of Lindbergh Lake, about eighty miles from here. It's this multiseasonal three-sectioned painting, so the artist would have needed to go there frequently to plan his work. Maybe he's there now."

"I've checked everywhere."

"But there's the Bob Marshall Wilderness Area nearby. People spend months in The Bob all alone."

"I'll consider it after we've settled your case. Do you think your lecturer would talk about the artist?"

"I'm sure he would. He bored me silly for a whole semester about other artists and they're dead."

Abruptly, Zane laughed. "Ouch! That's awfully critical, isn't it?"

"You're right." She smiled back.

She liked being around Zane.

His gaze drifted over her shoulder toward the front entrance. Suddenly, he stiffened. "Kristin, listen to me carefully," he whispered. "Take your purse and walk toward the washroom, but don't go in. Do it now!"

She opened her mouth, but his icy glare froze any questions. Lifting her purse, she slid out of the booth.

"Hurry, but don't run," he said quietly, taking a fake sip of water. "And don't look around."

A minute later, she found herself down the dim hall near the washrooms, her heart pounding. From the front of the restaurant, the sound of a loud crash bounced down to her.

She jumped. What was going on?

Suddenly, a dark blur raced toward her and propelled her into the restaurant's busy kitchen. Inside the steamy room, a young cook's eyes widened in shock.

Then someone slapped a hand over her mouth.

FOUR

"Hey!"

Kristin heard the young cook's sharp word, but immediately grabbed the hand that covered her mouth. Her nails, though short, dug into the hard muscle and dark hair. At the same time, the cook lunged for something in front of her.

Her assailant behind her leaned forward. "It's me, Zane! Stay still. Our friend here is trying to save both us and his soup."

She froze immediately, but did not turn. His grip on her was tight, his whole weight shifting them both away from the stove that stood so close to the door.

Finally, she looked down. The cook was busy steadying a large pot of steaming soup. Her flailing could have tipped it over onto her and Zane.

She blew out a sigh. Once the soup was safe on another burner, Zane released her.

She spun around. "What was that for? You could have made it a whole lot worse for both of us! Why not just tell me to come in here?"

"Sorry. I didn't see the soup, either, until it was nearly too late." He was steering her through the hot, fragrant kitchen, around the startled cook and his pot of soup. As they passed him, Zane shoved a pair of ten-dollar bills into the man's hand. "For our meal. Table eight. Thank you."

His left hand wrapped firmly around her elbow, his right hand flipping out his cell phone, he moved them swiftly through to the back door. "I needed to get you out of the hallway quickly and I didn't want us trapped in the washrooms," he continued. "Let's go, Kristin, I'll explain later."

They hurried outside. Zane threw a fast glance around them. Then, taking her arm, he led her around the corner of the restaurant.

Curious, Kristin leaned forward to peer back around the corner. The back door to the restaurant's kitchen opened, and out walked the cook. He scanned the back alley, then returned inside. A heavyset man with a swarthy face and dark scowl stepped out behind him.

Zane pulled her back. "*That* man walked in, sat at one of the front tables and watched you. As soon as we started to eat, he called someone. A minute later, another man came in, sat at another table. Both then got up and began to walk our way."

"Did you recognize them? Do you know them?"

"No, but I know they weren't there for the quesadillas. I saw the first one in front of the café this morning."

She gasped. "Are you sure?"

"Absolutely. I studied the crowd after you said you'd been pushed. Let's face it, if he was in that restaurant just to have a bite to eat, he wouldn't have followed us out the kitchen door, right?"

She bit her lip. Had he been the man who'd pushed her in front of the truck? "What else did he do?"

"When he reached into his jacket, I saw a gun. As soon

as you headed down that hall, I pulled a chair toward our booth, as if we were expecting company. The waitress ran into it, and spilled a drink. That pretty much delayed him from reaching us. That's when I followed you. You had your back to me and I needed you out of there immediately. I'm sorry if I was a bit rough. You struggled and were going to knock that hot soup all over yourself."

"You scared the daylights out of me." She sighed and leaned against the brick wall. "Are we going to call the police?"

"Just because we're suspicious doesn't mean they'll be. They think you imagined being pushed."

"I didn't imagine it."

After punching in some numbers, Zane brought his cell phone up to his ear. "This is Zane Black. I'm calling to let you know that there will be someone staying in my office for the next few days." He covered his phone. "This is my building's security service."

Irritated, Kristin listened to his call. What was he doing? Did he think she'd just go where he told her? As soon as his cell phone clicked shut, she spoke. "You want me to stay in your office?"

"I'm not going to take any chances here."

Someone around the corner of the building knocked over a garbage can, then swore loudly. Kristin jumped, and in the same moment, Zane dragged her down the alley. When they reached the main road, he hurried her into the next business, a sporting goods shop.

Standing behind a tall rack of windbreakers, she asked, "How will going to your office do any good?"

She remembered what Jackson's words had been that last night he saw her mother. Someone had learned the safe house's location. As a result, Eloise had to abandon her in order to keep her safe. How was Zane's office going to do what a federal safe house couldn't do?

"It's got excellent security. And before you say you don't need security, think. You attended the Martino trial because it was related to why your mother is in hiding. An FBI agent wants you to stop looking for her, probably because it's too dangerous for both of you. You need to be more than a little careful."

She remembered Jackson's words. The Martino family wanted to honor the old dying don. There was no way they could have learned where she lived. "But Jackson said that traveling around for a while would throw off any person who tried to follow me. And the security inside that courtroom was tight because the judge didn't want it turned into a sideshow. The spectators would have had to register before going in."

"Maybe someone has that list. And when he called, did Jackson warn you something might happen to you?"

"Yes. How did you know that?" she asked softly.

"I guessed it, based on all you've said, but now that you've told me, I can see I'm right." He pulled a face and glanced out the window again. "It's got something to do with your mother and Martino."

It was as if he could read her mind. Was she that transparent? "What else do you know?"

"I don't know enough about the trial, but I will by tomorrow morning. In the meantime, you need to stay somewhere safe, like my office. No arguments, either, okay? This is your life here, and if you die, you'll never find your mother."

Again, Zane looked out the front window of the store, toward the restaurant. She hated the way he'd manipulated her need to find her mother. And yet, he was so right.

She didn't want to die without ever finding her mother. Or worse, put her mother, the woman who'd done everything in her power to save her life, back into danger.

Her stomach growled. "Yeah, I know," she muttered to it. "Stress makes you hungry." She'd missed most of their lunch and it was showing.

Trying to ignore the pangs, she glanced outside herself at the main street in Westbrook. Zane's car was in a parking lot at the other side of the restaurant. To reach it they'd have to walk past the place.

Zane fished out his car keys. "Stay here. I'll get the car. I'd call a taxi, but I've been here two years—"

"And you've only ever seen one. I know. We have only one taxicab in this town. Everything is walking distance." She glanced at the approaching clerk before watching Zane leave.

Kristin hovered in the back of the store, declining the offer of assistance from the clerk. Within a few minutes, Zane reappeared and she quickly exited the store.

"I'm not going to your office, Zane," she said firmly.

"My office has everything you need."

"It's not that. I'm not fussy. It's just that you have a business to run, and I don't think those people who have hired you would appreciate a strange woman living in your office, even if all their personal information were secure. Why don't I go to a hotel in Kalispell?"

He considered her suggestion. "All right," he finally said. "I'll call and make the reservations." When he pointed to where his car was, he handed her his keys. "Go to the Broadview Hotel. Do you know it?"

She nodded. "But I need some things before I can go."

"No. Don't go home. I'll see to it that they provide whatever you need, a light lunch and some personal stuff.

The hotel is excellent at security, too, so use the valet service at the front entrance. Don't stop along the way, either."

Lifting her eyebrows, she took the keys. "Am I allowed to watch TV?"

"Don't be sarcastic, Kristin. This is for your own good. I'd rather err on the side of caution until I know all the facts here. Yes, it's probably better that you stay in Kalispell. I've got a lot of reading to do on the Martino family and I may not be able to do it all at home."

She hadn't expected Zane to agree to the hotel, and now that it was done, she found herself not wanting to give up her search for her mother. Not even for a day.

She looked at the keys he'd given her. "What about leaving you here without a car?"

"I have another one. I'll stop by the hotel tomorrow." As if on an impulse, he squeezed her hand. His fingers felt warm and comforting and she found herself wanting to cling to them. "I'm sorry for all that's happening to you, Kristin, but you need to take care of your own safety right now, and not to worry about anyone else." His voice dropped. "That includes your mother."

She looked up at him, seeing him strong and lean and in control, knowing the right thing to do. In that moment, she didn't want to leave.

Foolish notion, she told herself. Zane didn't need her breathing down his neck.

And yet, was she really doing the right thing here, trusting Zane?

Yes, he was trustworthy; she knew that because she'd checked his credentials before calling him.

"Go. I'll be there tomorrow morning." With a gentle shove, he directed her toward his car. She looked up at his face, but he was already scanning the area. She had no choice but to leave.

Zane didn't watch her leave. He watched everyone else, instead. But no one seemed interested in a woman trotting out to a run-of-the-mill car. Within the minute, Kristin had slipped from the parking space and driven away. He followed her taillights with his eyes until she turned and headed toward the highway, avoiding the center of Westbrook.

On his walk to retrieve his other car, he spotted the two men arguing outside the restaurant. He'd also seen the gun the bigger man carried. They continued to argue as they climbed into a car. He memorized the Illinois plate number.

Someone was after her, all right. And that someone was getting desperate.

Which meant that all his other work would have to cease immediately. Including dealing with that small lead she'd mentioned about the painting.

She shouldn't be looking for her mother at this time, either, but he wasn't sure he could convince her of that, certainly not when these circumstances seemed tied to the missing woman. He'd been lucky to get her to agree to the hotel. Hunger had probably weakened her resolve. He'd heard her stomach rumble, so the promise of a meal must have helped. Zane almost smiled at that thought.

But he grimaced instead as he walked to where he kept his second car. It looked as if he was taking her case, after all. He flipped open his cell and called his answering service, telling the woman to hold his calls, adding that he was going to be busy.

He had some homework to do, reading up on the Martino crime family and just how they might find out where Kristin lived.

* * *

The next morning, despite the long night he'd put in, Zane headed into Kalispell. Entering the hotel, he spied Kristin stepping off the elevator. When their gazes locked, she offered up a guilty smile. "I was hungry, and the room-service breakfast was just coffee and cold toast."

He tried a frown, but it wouldn't form. Her soft, gently contrite smile repelled any anger at her for slipping out of her room. "Let's go, then. The restaurant serves a decent breakfast."

They sat at a far table by the window that faced a series of grid-line streets. At the end of the budding trees and short buildings, he spied the downtown mall. Zane could see both outside and through the restaurant entrance to the front desk. Their food arrived, a full breakfast of fresh pastries, boiled eggs, that great coffee they had here and juice.

Zane watched as Kristin helped herself to food and a large mug of coffee. Montanans loved their coffee, and since coming here, he'd learned why. It *was* good.

"Last night," he began, accepting a cup from her, "I checked in to the recent Martino trial. That woman you spoke to, Olivia Jarrod, did a bang-up job at testifying. She's a brave woman, especially considering she's pregnant and her husband had been shot saving her life. You've got to admire that kind of strength."

"I knew she was strong when I met her that day in Jackson's office. My mother had that kind of strength, too, because she had to leave me after an attempt on her life. That was hard for her."

"Did Jackson tell you that?"

Her chin wrinkled and she deliberately took a mouthful of food. To avoid answering, he noted. It was difficult, he knew it, and though he should be pushing her for more info, as he would have done anyone else, he couldn't. She was hurting too much.

Give her time, he told himself. *She'll talk.* Last night, as he'd read up on the Martino family, and between phone calls to his contacts out east, he'd thought and rethought about Kristin's need to find her mother and her fear of telling anyone about it. As much as that need and that fear were at odds with each other, he knew Kristin would find a way to partner them together. She had that kind of inner determination.

But being told by the FBI to back off was odd. There had to be a good reason for it.

As he began to frown, Kristin's cell phone rang. She answered it, then after listening to the caller, she covered the microphone part.

"That's my father's law partner. He says that he has a large letter from me. He's going up to Westbrook anyway, and wants to drop it off at my house."

"How well do you know him?"

"He's the son of my father's previous law partner and he practices in Missoula now. My father handled the cases up in Westbrook. I've known him all my life. Well, practically all my life."

Zane didn't like the idea of the man dropping by Kristin's house. "Have him deliver it to my office. He can shove it in my mail slot by the front door. Were you expecting it?"

She looked thoughtful. "I've been searching for my mother for months, and sending out letters, too. It could be an answer. I had used my father's work address and I am expecting a photo of my mother."

"It could be important, then."

She nodded, then told the lawyer where to drop off the letter. After hanging up, she said, "He sounded suspicious, and said he's on his way to Westbrook. He must wonder why I'm having him drop it off at a private investigative office. The letter should be in your slot by later this morning."

"Good, we can enjoy our breakfast, then."

They lingered over their meal, with Zane asking her questions about her youth. A nice, enviable youth, he noted. The kind other kids had, not him. Not the kind he and his adoptive sisters had.

Had he been adopted because his parents had no boys? Was life before he came along easier, before his adoptive father became abusive, believing that was how God wanted fathers to be? Or was it an excuse? Kristin's upbringing was so very different and yet they both had much in common.

Finally, after the last of the coffee was drank, they left. Before long, were out on the road, returning to Westbrook, only a few minutes drive away from Kalispell.

They reached Zane's office building shortly after. Just west of the town, it had a beautiful view of the surrounding mountains. Out front of the main entrance, a series of delivery slots had been built into the wall by the locked front door. Zane let them in, then unlocked his mail slot. Among some other envelopes was a large brown one, stiff with cardboard inside, he expected.

Kristin looked at the return address before smiling. "I know what this is. Remember I said I'd found a woman in Chicago who ran a foster home? She remembers my mother, even remembers that my mother told her she was pregnant."

"Did your mother ever contact her?"

"No." She shrugged. "All she had was this picture of the children there at the time, with their names on the back, and she was willing to send it to me. I just jumped on the chance to get a picture of my mother when she was younger than I am now."

The old photograph probably wouldn't be much help. He wasn't sure what it could tell them, apart from what the woman looked like more than twenty years ago. But it was important to Kristin, he could see.

"How did you know where to look for this foster home?" he asked, watching her study the package.

"Jackson told me the name of the place. It wasn't that hard to track down. Finding the address of the woman who ran it was harder, but I used some of Dad's eastern contacts."

She was resourceful, if nothing else. Zane watched her slide out a large photograph and hold it between them so they could both see it. It was surprisingly good quality, clear and crisp with bright colors, even after all these years.

He pointed to a young woman in the back row. "That's your mom right there, I bet. She looks just like you."

"You think? Her face is thinner."

"Remember she's about, what, four years younger than you are now?"

Nodding, Kristin flipped the photo over. The woman who'd taken the shot had been diligent in writing down all the children's names. Zane scanned the top row and found what he was looking for.

"Eloise Hill," he murmured. "I told you it was her."

He'd barely finished speaking when Kristin flipped the photo back, studied the faces, and then flipped the photo to the back again.

"What's wrong?" he asked.

She showed him the photo, pointing not to the slim girl in the back row, who was not tall enough for the place, but probably put there to hide her pregnancy. No, Kristin was pointing to the gangly youth who towered beside her.

"I know who this man is. And I know where he lives."

FIVE

Kristin's heart pounded fast as she stared at the boy beside her mother.

"Who is it?" Zane asked.

"Clay West. Well, I don't know him per se, but I do know his fiancée, Violet Kramer. She's a reporter in Missoula who wrote an article on a woman trying to do the right things in her life. A kind of redemption story. What was *her* name?" She thought for a moment. "Gwyn something. It caught my interest when I was searching the newspaper's archives, and so I've been reading her stories regularly since. I even called her editor not long ago to tell him how much I enjoyed her articles. I had tried to call her, but she was out of the office."

"And she's engaged to Clay West?"

"Yes. I saw their announcement online last week. It mentions that Clay was from Chicago."

Zane peered deeply into the photograph. "That kid looks about fourteen. Are you sure it's him?"

"I'm positive. The announcement mentioned that his parents were deceased and that he had lived at the Southside Foster Home in Chicago. That's where my mother lived, but I wasn't sure if their time there overlapped so I didn't say anything. This looks like a younger version of him, all right."

She pulled out her phone and clicked a few buttons. "I still have Violet's work number in my history. Here it is. She'll know where I can find Clay."

Violet Kramer answered on the third ring. "Kramer."

Kristin quickly introduced herself, keeping the reason as concise as possible. "I need some information. I'm looking for my mother, Eloise Hill, and I have just realized that your fiancé knew her."

Violet went quiet. Kristin knew immediately that she'd hit the nail on the head. Finally, the feisty newswoman answered, "How did you find this out?"

"The woman from the Southside Foster Home sent me a photograph, which has both Clay and my mom in it, though my mom was ready to age out at the time. Shortly after that, she gave birth to me, and about a year later, she disappeared." Kristin clung to her cell phone. *Please, Lord, have her help me.*

"And you're calling me to locate Clay?"

"I saw your engagement announcement in the paper and I don't know if your editor told you but I've… well…I've been following your articles since you wrote about that Gwyn woman. I don't know how else to contact Clay."

There was a short pause. "Kristin, I strongly urge you to rethink your search for your mother. Forget about her. I know that's going to be hard, but believe me, it's a whole lot safer for you and for your mother if you just drop your search completely."

Kristin's heart sank. "I have a right to know my mother."

Violet softened. "I understand. But believe me, it can get you killed. And get your mother killed, too. When a person is put into the Witness Protection Program, it's for a good reason. Mainly their own safety."

Kristin felt irritation rise in her. "I could save my mother's life if I can find her. She saved mine once. This is the least I can do for her."

"No, you can't save her life. I used to think that way, too," she answered, her tone sharper. "I always thought that I could help people by disclosing the truth, but instead, I learned to trust the people in law enforcement. They know the right things to do."

Kristin had no idea what Violet's words meant. What had changed her mind? Her fiancé? The reporter sounded as if she'd learned her lessons the hard way.

She pulled in her breath and answered, "I understand. I know the risks. In fact, I've been face-to-face with them."

Violet's tone changed immediately. "What do you mean?"

So the woman was as sharp as she suspected. She scrambled to say something innocuous. "Nothing. In fact, it was probably just a coincidence."

"What could be a coincidence? What happened to you, Kristin?"

She sighed and leaned back against the wall in the quiet foyer, avoiding Zane's deepening frown. "I was pushed into traffic. I don't know if was an accident or not." Kristin held back the part of the swarthy men following her into that restaurant, preferring to keep the details to a minimum.

"If your mother is hiding from the Mob, like most in the program are, you need to stop searching for her *now*," Violet snapped. "These men aren't playing a game here."

"I know. But I also know that my only link to my mother right now is your fiancé. I thought I could get a hold of you more easily than him. That maybe, after seeing that article you wrote, you'd understand and have him call me."

She was sounding desperate, but right then, she decided she needed to be firm. "Violet, Clay has met my mother. I'd like to talk to him. And after this winter, when my parents died, I've learned not to wait for a better, safer time. Because sometimes, it doesn't come."

Kristin held her breath. She'd so rarely been this bold, and Violet was everything she wasn't—smart, feisty and yet feminine.

But this was too important. "Haven't you ever lost someone dear to you?"

Finally, Violet spoke. "I'll ask Clay, but I can't guarantee he'll agree to talk to you. That time in the foster home was tough. He struggled after his parents died. He told me how Eloise made him feel welcome, and how she taught him to rise above life's circumstances. Because of your mother's courage, he decided to go into law enforcement."

Hope flared in her. Clay sounded like a man with integrity. Surely, he'd talk to her. "I understand," she answered.

The woman hung up, and slowly, Kristin closed her own phone. She turned to Zane. "So we see if he calls me back."

She looked down again at the envelope. "Imagine a man who knew my mother ending up in Montana. I hope he can help me."

Again, biting her lip, she found herself marveling at God's hand. *I am with you always.* That verse was in the Bible, and today, it was taking on a stronger meaning.

"This guy, Clay, was just another kid at that foster home. Your mother had her problems, and I imagine Clay did, too. And the overlap time they were there could have been only a few days."

Before she could answer, her phone rang. The soft music she'd loved so much when she'd chosen that ringtone now cut her to the quick. "It must be him."

She took a deep breath and answered the phone. "Hello?"

"Kristin Perry?"

She guessed the deep voice immediately. "Clay West, I presume?"

"Yes. Violet just called me. I'm sorry that you've had a scare. Did you call Jackson? He would want to know."

How did this police officer know Jackson? "No. But that's not why I called. I have a photograph from Gladys Burrows, the woman who ran the foster home you lived in. I saw your name in the engagement announcement and hoped you were one and the same."

"Violet thought it would be uplifting to have the foster home's name mentioned in the announcement."

She blew out a relieved sigh. He sounded willing to talk. "Do you remember the photo being taken?"

"Barely. It wasn't the best time in my life. I'd just lost my parents."

Kristin found herself nodding. "We've all had our rough spots. But you know why I'm calling. I need to find my mother, now more than ever."

"I don't know where she is, Kristin. Jackson asked me that once, too, but I haven't seen her since shortly after that picture was taken."

She'd steeled herself against that answer. "I know. But maybe you know something that can be helpful to me. Anything at all."

"I don't. You should be leaving this up to Jackson. He's doing his best to find your mother."

"I know, but I can't just sit and wait," she answered.

"You'll have to."

Kristin tightened her jaw. "Clay, you're one of the few people who knew my mother. I've recently lost my adoptive parents and I have absolutely no one left in this world.

Even if I don't go looking for my mother, it would mean the world to me to talk to someone who knew her. Please, Clay, this is important to me."

Clay had been there at that foster home. He was orphaned or, at the very least, abandoned. Like she felt right now. He of all people must have known what it felt like.

"All I want to do is talk to you, Clay," she choked out, hating that the tears were starting again, and how it could sound like she was sobbing and crying fake tears to manipulate him.

"I'm sorry," she added hastily. "I don't mean to sound so desperate."

There was another long pause. "It's okay. Even Violet has been shaken up by all that has happened, so I can imagine you'd be, too." He sighed. "I doubt I can help you find your mother, and you should call Jackson, but if you want, we can meet."

He didn't sound hopeful, but she'd take what she was offered. "Today?"

"Sure." He suggested a coffee shop close to the police station in downtown Missoula. After hanging up, she sniffed. "Sorry. I didn't mean to get all blubbery."

Zane watched her closely. "It's okay. So, he's agreed to meet you?"

"Yes." She gave him the address, all the while wondering at the same time if she'd shoved any tissues into her purse. She couldn't remember.

"It's been a long time since they were at that foster home. He probably can't be of any help."

"I don't care. I'll take anything right now."

"What about Jackson? He knew your mother. She trusted him enough to give you to him."

She nodded. "Yes. He won't say much about her, but I

get the feeling that the connection they shared was special, too." Her heart constricted at that thought. Had they been in love? How long had they known each other? They must have both been very young when Eloise got pregnant. Had they been intimate?

"Kristin, Jackson sounds like he's protecting you—"

She snapped her head around. "Yes, I know! Everyone wants to protect me." Her tone turned mocking. "Everyone tells me to trust Jackson, and not to do anything on my own, as if—"

Her cell phone's ring cut off her words. Scowling, she grabbed it and flipped it open. No ID available. Was this Clay canceling the meeting after having second thoughts?

"Hello?"

"Kristin?"

Kristin sagged. It was Jackson. She should have realized that Clay West would call the FBI agent the second he hung up. "Yes, Jackson?" she said for Zane's benefit.

"Why didn't you call me when you got pushed into traffic?"

Word got around pretty quick, she thought dismally. Of course, she didn't have to think hard at who had told Jackson. "It just happened yesterday. The police here say I was mistaken."

"Any witnesses?"

"No one who's talking. Everyone says they only saw me stumble."

She knew she should mention the men who'd followed them into the restaurant, but held back on that. She had no proof she'd been pushed, and no proof that the men at the restaurant wanted to hurt her. Jackson would need facts and evidence, not suspicions, even from a reliable source like Zane.

Irritation in his voice ground through the phone. "Did anything I said yesterday sink in?"

"Yes, but what am I supposed to do?" she answered back, feeling the frustration rise in her. "Just stand up, dust myself off and go home?"

"Exactly."

A thought hit her. "A bump into traffic hardly sounds like a Mob hit."

"Gunning people down may be the method of choice, but these men will take any opportunity that presents itself. Look, I'm coming to Montana in a couple of days. I expect you to lie low, stay put and not look for your mother." He definitely sounded angry. "Your parents protected you for a reason. Homeschooling, unlisted numbers, only the safest activities. They weren't just for your father's law practice. But you reporting what happened could have jeopardized all of that. Do you understand?"

How did Jackson know she'd been homeschooled, and that her parents had rarely let her out of their sight? "No, I don't understand. I was pushed into traffic and you are telling me to do nothing? What's going on? You aren't telling me everything. You say that this Martino guy has escaped custody and is looking for my mom and me. So how can my searching for her endanger her? If I'm dis- creet, and careful, they won't know. And for that matter, who's not to say that Martino isn't following you, in *your* search for my mother?"

She cut off her argument, hating that it came spilling out of her so suddenly. "I'm sorry, Jackson. I don't mean to take it out on you."

He, too, softened immediately. "I understand. I really do. You must also understand that I have more training than you do and I have more resources available to me. I'm coming out there, so please hang on. I'll update you then. I promise."

She blinked. "Okay."

She hung up shortly after, turning to Zane as she clicked shut her phone. "I'm expected to hang on, and do nothing. He's coming out here and will explain everything."

"And your meeting with Clay West?"

The thought of canceling it tightened around her chest, but she couldn't sit home. And talking to a police officer that obviously had called the FBI agent moments ago wasn't going to jeopardize her mother's safety. Clay West would just be reminiscing about the past. That was hardly looking for her mother. Surely, she'd be safe talking to a police officer half a block from the police station?

Kristin set her jaw and lifted her eyebrows. "I'm going to Missoula this afternoon. Want to come?"

"I should put my mail in my office first. I haven't been here for two days."

Relief washed through her. "I know I'm crazy to ask you this again, but does this mean you're taking on my case?"

He paused, looking as if he was giving himself one last chance to back out. Then, his eyes turning a cooler, steely color, he said, "Only if you tell me everything, not bits and pieces of nice, safe information. Are you willing to trust me now?"

She wet her lips. *Lord, should I? He's not a believer, but he sounds sincere.*

"I'm serious, Kristin. I know that Jackson warned you not to say much, but that's my deal. Either that or I call that FBI agent and tell him you're doing as you please."

She studied his face, trying to size up his threat. "He'd be here in a flash, you know," she whispered.

"That's my deal. Take it or leave it."

What choice did she really have? She had no desire to travel down to Missoula alone, and so far, Zane *had* shown his desire to help her. Nothing was going to come of her refusing to tell him everything.

She ran her fingers through her hair, smoothing down the side of the white scar, all the time throwing a swift glance around the entrance. Several people were leaving the office building. "Okay. But, Zane, I don't know much more than what I told you."

"Let me worry about that. You'd be surprised what rehashing things can do for the memory. You may know more than you realize."

She smiled. Zane could talk with Clay West.

"Don't be smiling like I've promised you the world, Kristin. Because there are still two men out there who appear to want you dead."

Her smile fell as they walked toward the small elevator. Zane was right. Clay may not know anything. So all the brilliant questions in the world wouldn't do any good.

And she'd be no further ahead in her search. Even Jackson hadn't been able to find Eloise.

Her heart lurched as she considered why that could be. Had those Martino mobsters found her mother first? And besides that, how was it that Jackson knew so much about her?

The elevator door slid open at the second floor and she stepped out. "I was just thinking of something. Jackson knew I was homeschooled. I wonder how."

"How would he have known your parents?"

"I don't know. All he said was that he arranged for them to adopt me. They must have been friends or something, but they never mentioned him and he never visited. Just another thing I don't know, yet."

"You can ask Jackson next time you're talking to him."

She felt her eyes sting. "I don't know if I even want to talk to him anymore, even if he promises to answer my questions. He doesn't know where my mother is, and he tells me I'm in danger. I want to find my mother, but he keeps discouraging me from doing so." She bit her lip. "I can't stand the thought of not ever being able to meet her. I only just learn that she exists, right after my parents die, and then, I'm told to leave it all alone and wait until some distant time? It's not fair."

Gone. Her parents, a mother that she so suddenly needed to find. All gone. She was expected just to carry on with her life. She started to walk again, following the little sign that discreetly pointed toward Zane's office. She could feel his gaze on her back, and wondered what he thought of her. She missed being loved and cared about, but it would be sheer foolishness to expect understanding from Zane.

Even though she wanted so desperately to know someone cared for her. Kristin found herself at a standstill in front of his office door, her feet heavy and her eyes beginning to water. *Again.*

Mom and Dad, I miss you.

Feeling foolish, she dug through her purse for a tissue, actually finding one this time, but her shaking hands couldn't hang on to it. The tissue drifted to the floor in a still, dim hallway.

"Here." Zane stooped to retrieve it.

"Thanks," she mumbled, reaching out her hand to take it. "I'm sorry. I was thinking of how much my parents had protected me. They must have thought they were doing the right thing, but I guess they hadn't counted on…" She sniffled. "You know, dying…"

She reached out for the tissue Zane held. Where was it?

But he didn't hand it up to her. Instead, he stared at his door. She held out her hand, but he didn't move.

"What's wrong?"

"My door is scratched. Mostly around the lock, but—" He cut off his sentence.

She blinked back her tears and peered at him. "But what?"

"Back up, Kristin. Nice and slowly."

She obeyed, taking only one step.

"No, more. Two more, then turn and walk down the stairs and straight out the building and call 911."

"What's going on, Zane?"

He stared up at her, a somber look on his face. "My office door has been rigged to blow up."

SIX

Kristin gasped. "Blow up! What do you mean?"

"Explode. It's got a trip wire strung across the bottom of the door. Someone has broken in and set something on the other side, and I don't think it's to turn on the lights. Now, do as I say. If you meet anyone else, tell them to leave the building immediately."

"What if they don't listen?"

"Just go, Kristin! Go!" Still bent down, he tipped his head to peer at the door more closely.

"What about you?"

"Go!"

She backed up a few more feet, hating her suddenly nervous chatter. At the stairs beside the elevator, she stopped and turned, ripping her watery vision from Zane. He hadn't moved, merely stared at the trip wire, his right hand still holding that tissue that had probably saved their lives.

Then he slowly straightened, and she pushed open the stairwell door, all the while yanking out her cell phone.

Her shaking hands wouldn't punch out those three easy numbers. Instead, as she hurried to the back of the parking lot, she struggled just to hold the stupid phone still.

A hand behind her reached for her phone and she jumped.

Zane took her phone and dialed the emergency number, the whole time guiding them past the parking lot onto a strip of grass some fifty feet or more from the building. Over her pounding heart, she barely heard him explain what they'd found, that there were others still inside. Zane calmly stated everything.

Zane continued to use the phone, calling people. It took a few minutes for her to realize he was calling those who rented other offices to ensure everyone got out of the building.

The wind lifted his straight dark hair as he turned a full circle, checking out the surroundings. Satisfied by something, he led her behind a small storage hut close to the next building. The wind released his hair when they rounded the corner.

She swallowed. His office had been sabotaged? Someone wanted Zane dead? Was it because of her?

A nudge drew her back to reality. She looked down at her arm to find Zane was returning her cell phone. "Is there anyone left in the building?" she asked.

"No. I called everyone."

She looked toward the building, seeing others exiting quickly. In the distance, sirens grew louder with each ticking second. As she turned, her gaze collided with Zane's. He had such beautiful eyes. The color was cool, as sharp as blue could be, and yet there was a warmth she couldn't describe. A haunting warmth borne of worry and concern.

He cared for people. She reached out and touched his arm. "It's okay. The police will know what to do. They'll save your office and they'll—"

He shook his head. "I don't care about my office. I was

thinking that we could have both died. And so could have a lot of innocent people."

"Thank God we didn't."

His short, hesitant glance came with a flick of dark eyebrows. "Yes, one might thank Him. But it's more—"

He stopped, as if censoring his own words. She couldn't ask him to finish his sentence. The police van had arrived, an officer leaping from the passenger side to tell them to back up farther. The other officer approached Zane to ask where he thought the bomb was.

Eventually, the firefighters from Kalispell pulled in with a hazardous materials trailer. Someone dressed in what looked like a brown space suit entered the building. It seemed as though everyone was holding a full collective breath. Half an hour later, the space suit guy walked out of the building with a round metal ball. He set it into another machine in the trailer. Everyone around them cheered.

Kristin hugged herself tightly, watching as she backed into the next building, listening as Zane eventually gave his statement, watching until finally, thankfully, it was all over. Zane then told her that they were going to the police station to offer fingerprints so the police could eliminate them should they be able to lift some from the building.

A car pulled up, its side door logo telling them the reporters from Westbrook's paper had arrived. Zane grabbed Kristin's arm and steered her away from the commotion. "Let's go. I don't feel like answering any more questions right now."

She nodded. The police had intercepted the reporter, and onlookers who'd gravitated to the scene were more than willing to offer their opinions. Before the reporter could even look for them, Kristin and Zane were gone.

After a few minutes, Zane parked near the police

station, a busy place where several cars filled the visitor spots. On the way, she called to delay her meeting with Clay by a couple of hours. "After this, we'll head down to Missoula," Zane said after listening to her call. "It's best that we steer clear of the action."

After they gave and signed their statements, Zane asked the officer, a different one than the one who'd taken her statement yesterday, "That vest that was brought in yesterday, the one belonging to Kristin Perry, has it been processed yet?"

The man looked confused. "The one from the woman who says she was pushed into traffic?"

Heat rose in Kristin's face as she leaned forward. "I *was* pushed. Did you find out what that stuff was on it? It looked like there were two smudges from two hands."

"It was checked, but there's nothing on it, I'm afraid. I'll get it to show you."

He returned a moment later with her vest. And flipped the vest repeatedly.

There were no grease marks on it at all.

Gaping, Kristin spread the vest out across the desk between her and the police officer. "Someone has cleaned this!"

Zane took the vest and sniffed the back. "It's got a solvent smell to it." He peered up at the police officer. "Who checked it out?"

"I was asked to do the prelim on it. That's how I found it. There was nothing to lift off. Are you sure there were smudges on it?"

"Of course there were," Kristin answered tightly. "Or else the police officer would never have taken it and wasted the resources. Who has had access to this?"

The officer didn't answer. Zane smiled briefly at

Kristin, the expression in his eyes saying, *You go, girl.* He turned to the police officer. "You've been busy here today."

The man folded his arms. "Yes, but I can't tell you who has been here, if that's what you're asking."

"No, but you do know who might have had access to that evidence. Even if they're not allowed to. And you have security cameras, so why not check them?"

The police officer looked over Zane's shoulders at a pair of middle-aged men who had just entered. ID cards dangled from lanyards around their necks. The men walked past them, as Zane turned to watch, though not before looking knowingly at the officer in front of him, Kristin noted. The officer then watched the two visitors carefully.

She curbed a smile. Zane had done enough to plant the seed of doubt in the officer's mind. She leaned over the counter. "Can I take my vest, then, if you're done with it?"

"Of course. I'm sorry it wasn't useful."

She signed a sheet to accept her vest, watching out of the corner of her eye at Zane. He kept a close eye on the men as they were allowed to pass into the rear of the station. She followed his stare, noticing one of the men had a slight limp and the other wore a smug expression. When they reached the back offices, one man turned to meet her curious gaze.

His short gray hair and heavyset frame didn't seem out of place. He must be another police officer. She frowned. At this distance, across the busy room, she didn't recognize him. Yet, he looked right at her as if he recognized *her*....

Oh, good grief, he was probably thinking she was that nutcase college student who thought she'd been pushed into traffic.

Embarrassed, she looked away, grabbed her vest and muttered her thanks. Outside, she rolled up the vest and tucked it under her arm.

Even Zane seemed preoccupied, as he led her to his car and clicked the unlock button tersely. After they climbed in, he turned to her. "Someone cleaned your vest."

"I know. But why?"

"I don't know. Did you notice those other men?"

"They probably think I'm that crazy girl who thinks someone is after her. Did you catch their names?"

"No. I think they're U.S. Marshals." He tightened his lips.

Kristin's eyes widened. "What would the U.S. Marshals be doing here?"

"Among other things, U.S. Marshals are responsible for rounding up fugitives from justice. And remember that Martino is a fugitive now."

"So everyone knows to be on the lookout for him, then."

"Absolutely. He's making national news, and some show on TV is doing a special on his escape, hoping someone will help to locate him. But their reason for being here may not have anything to do with us."

"Good thing we're going to Missoula and not hanging around just in case it does."

He ran his tongue along his lips, staring ahead of him, out the windshield. "Indeed."

"Zane? Do *you* honestly believe that Martino is after me?" When he didn't answer, she pressed further. "I deserve to know. Don't try to shelter me, Zane. I got that all my life from my parents, but I'm not a child anymore."

"The truth isn't all sugary and sweet, Kristin, like your life has been. Christians like to see life that way, but it's not, and I don't know if you're ready for that."

She gaped at him. She opened her mouth to speak, but held back. He was right. She'd been sheltered and cared for and shown God's love in a warm, loving environment.

She gulped back her revelation. Had she actually thought she could handle real life?

Suddenly, she didn't want to be shielded from the world. "Yes, I'm ready. My mother gave me up for adoption and disappeared to save my life. My parents kept the letter she wrote to Jackson, maybe to prove to me that the world wasn't safe. When they thought I was ready to hear that."

"Do you have the letter on you?"

"No, it's in the file I found in my father's safe, now in my father's filing cabinet at home. Jake is still repairing the safe. He had to drill into the side of it, in order to figure the combination with this tiny camera we had. Now he has to fill the hole in, sand it down and repaint it. I told him not to hurry with that. There was no point."

"I'd like to see that file."

"Most of it seems to be records of business trips. I can hardly make any sense out of it, but I haven't sat down and tried, either. I told you I don't know much more about my biological mother. What do you expect to find?"

He didn't answer right away. He leaned forward to start the engine, and then stopped, staring at the keys.

"Zane?"

"After we left the restaurant, I called my office building's security to tell them that you'd be staying there. We heard someone lurking around the corner of the restaurant. Then I said it again in that sporting goods shop. Someone must have overheard me and thought you'd be the next person going to my office."

"Someone must have known you, then."

"That's quite possible. I'm the only private investigator in a small town. And I did a talk for the high-school students on a career day. Lots of people know who I am."

"What are you getting at?"

"They were expecting you at my office, not me." He looked grim. "That bomb was for you, Kristin. And these people don't care who they kill at the same time."

SEVEN

"How is that possible? I mean, from the time you wanted me to go to your office to the time we got there was how long?"

"Remember, I didn't go into my office yesterday. I got my second car and then went home to do my research. Whoever did this had nearly twenty hours. My office is the last down the hall on a floor that isn't busy. And the bomb was a pretty simple device, not hard to put together." He looked grim. "Kristin, Vincent Martino escaped custody and it's logical to assume that he wants Eloise dead. Maybe they did follow you here from the trial?"

"They had plenty of opportunity to kill me on my trip through New England. Even climbing Mount Katahdin in Maine, there were times when I was separated from my friend, and they could have killed me then. If they followed me here, they would have had plenty of time to kill me before now."

"Then someone only recently got the list of who would be allowed in the court. Or else more people than you realize know you're adopted. Jake maybe? He opened your safe for you."

"No. He left me alone before I actually opened the safe door."

"What about your minister?"

She pulled a face. "He's too young to have been around when I came to Westbrook."

"But some of the older parishioners must remember when they brought you home."

Kristin paused. "My mom and dad moved from Billings shortly after they adopted me. For a while, Dad kept an office there with his partner, but later opened one here. Then after his partner died, his new partner moved the other office to Missoula. Everyone at church must assume I'm a change-of-life baby."

"Perhaps that's why your parents moved. New people, fresh start. But your father's law partner would have known, right?"

"There may be people in Billings who know I'm adopted, but they haven't said anything. I got a few cards, but no one mentioned it. I should call the pastor there sometime…" She let her words die away.

He looked deep in thought. "It's odd that Billings is where you were adopted from, and where your family lived before, and also where the U.S. Marshals are located."

She shrugged. "Billings is a big city."

"Billings," he repeated.

"What about it?"

He muttered something, then shrugged. "I don't know." He smiled at her, but even Kristin knew it was forced. "We need to get out of Westbrook for a little while." His smile widened. "We'll find your mother, Kristin. It'll all work out."

"I hope so. I've been praying for this to all work out. And I know you don't pray, but things happen for a reason. Surely, you believe that?"

"They do, but the reason isn't always God, Kristin. Things happen when people do stupid things. Or cruel, selfish things."

"Then God will use those things to His Glory. I'm not saying that God will make everything rosy for me, or sugarcoated so I don't have to suffer, but He'll make things work out for the best. Not my best, but His best."

"Then how can Christians go on with life if they know there's going to be pain caused by God?"

"God doesn't cause the pain. He allows it because He knows there's something better waiting for those of us who trust Him, when we leave this earth. Pain is tough, but God is tougher. Don't you think that maybe we're on a journey? Doesn't this feel like that to you?"

He didn't answer. They were already on the highway by this time, and the easy driving gave him the time to consider Kristin's question. If she hadn't begun to cry at that moment in front of his office, and dropped that tissue, he wouldn't have stooped to pick it up and wouldn't have seen the bomb.

She was tenderhearted and protected by loving parents, and it was that flaw, though he shouldn't call it a flaw, that saved their lives back there in front of his office door.

Even meeting Kristin did have a fateful feel to it. She had offered an unusual lead in his own search for his brother, one that hadn't been seen before. He'd known that a man named Kendall had studied at the university, but he hadn't stuck around after his courses. Zane had talked to his professor, but none said anything about any donated paintings. This last lead, one on Kendall's lodgings while here, hadn't panned out, either. But Kristin's lead was promising.

If this was all happening for a reason, then that meant that Someone was guiding them.

God? Did He really care that much for him? If so, where was He when Zane was a kid getting a beaten?

"So," he asked, shoving away those disconcerting thoughts, "tell me what you know about your birth mother. Even the things you've figured out or just suspected."

She blew out a sigh. "There's not much. Her name was Eloise Hill, but Jackson believes she's changed it. She was in the Witness Protection Program because she'd witnessed a Mob murder. Then the Mob found her. Jackson told me the story. She was holding me one day, when there was this explosion, and a piece of shrapnel literally burned between us. Since my scar is on the right side of my head, and her scar is on the right side, too, I must have been looking over my mother's shoulder. It did more damage to me than to my mother, I'm told."

"So your mother just abandoned you?"

She shot him a hot look. "She left one night, but not before shoving a note in the mobile above my crib. We were at a safe house when the Mob found us. Jackson was also there at the time and that next night woke up when I started to cry. After a bit, he knew no one was helping me, so he got up and found me with that note. He took me back to Chicago, and then found a Christian couple to take me."

"But they lived in Billings, right?"

"Yes, Jackson got a new birth certificate for me that stated that I was born in Billings, but my parents also kept the old one. They must have wanted to tell me someday, or hoped to find Eloise."

"So she must have given the real birth certificate to Jackson before she left."

"She gave everything on me to Jackson. I guess she was on the run and was scared the Mafia would find her with my birth certificate and connect her to me. For my sake, she decided to break all ties."

"What's your father's name?"

"The birth registry lists him as Danny Douglas, but it's a bit confusing. I don't know if Eloise married him or not. He worked for the Martino family, and Jackson says he died trying to save my mother's life. It's all a bit vague, and sometimes Jackson is…well, it's as if he's hesitant to say too much about it. I get the feeling that he's holding something back."

"Could it be that he is your real father?"

She looked shocked, briefly, before her brows met in a soft frown. "I hadn't thought of that before. I don't know very much about that time."

"What else did Jackson say?"

She shrugged. "He thought I had some of my mother's mannerisms." Abruptly, she laughed, sadly almost, he thought.

Zane grimaced. How could Jackson McGraw deny her the opportunity to find her mother, without offering any sympathy? And yet he sounded as though he really cared for her.

Her search would have to be far more dangerous than he and Kristin realized.

And, as he felt his jaw tighten, he knew he didn't want anything to happen to her at all.

Beside him, Kristin rubbed her forehead. She looked as if she might be getting a headache. He needed a break, too. He needed to clear his head with some fresh air. Cool mountain air would bring about that professional distance he needed to have.

Ahead was a rest stop, complete with gas station, playground, small restaurant and gift shop. Zane hit the signal light. "We need a break," he said gruffly.

Sniffling, she nodded. "I've never been to so many restaurants in my life." Her soft words cut into him, and he disliked how much they hurt. They'd only known each other a day and a half, he reminded himself. She'd done a one-eighty on trusting him, but that didn't mean he should treat her differently from any other client.

Most clients wanted him to check on cheating spouses or investigate untrustworthy employees. Suddenly, he hated his job. So much distrust. Maybe because he'd been so jaded by his childhood that he figured he could handle the suspicions needed in this line of work. Now his suspicions irked him. He hated to feel guilty.

He turned in and parked in front of the restaurant. Slowly, Kristin climbed out. She stood with her hand on the roof of his car, turning carefully as she looked up at the mountains, then down to the restaurant, and over to the gas pumps. They'd already passed the small town of Condon, and the road had straightened out to a simple stretch of narrow valley nestled between the mountains.

"Is there something wrong?" he asked her as he closed the driver's door.

She swallowed. "I've been here before."

EIGHT

Kristin had climbed out of Zane's car slowly, her mouth open as she stared around her. The line of snowy peaks to the left were closer than the ones to the right, and the whole valley acted like a wind tunnel, causing her to pull her jacket closer. The snow was gone from the last time she'd been to this gas station, but she knew this place.

Her heart pounded faster in her throat. *Oh, yes, she knew this place.* And its horrible memories. "I've been here before," she repeated.

"You've lived here most of your life. Of course you know this place."

"It's more than that." Giving one more glance at the snowy peaks around her, she hurried into the restaurant.

Inside, she walked around as Zane ordered a couple of coffees at the lunch counter. After scanning the small gift shop area, its trinkets and tourist clothing, she slid onto the round seat beside him at the counter, all the while gazing about.

An older man, vaguely familiar to her, approached carrying a coffeepot. She leaned forward. "Excuse me, but have we met before?"

The man peered at her, shaking his head slowly. "I don't think so."

"Was there a car accident nearby back in January?" She tried to keep her voice even, but couldn't. It wobbled as she finished her thoughts. "A husband and wife killed?"

The man's expression lit up as he pointed at her with his free hand. "Of course! I remember you. The police were with you." He frowned. "They were your folks that died, weren't they?"

She nodded before looking at Zane beside her. "I thought I remembered this place, but for some reason, I thought it happened down around Polson."

"That's on the other side of the Mission Mountains," Zane said, pointing to the rear of the restaurant where the stunning view was visible through a back window. "That's on Highway 93. This is Highway 83."

"You *were* pretty upset," the waiter added gently. "I don't blame you for getting that mixed up."

She pursed her lips, then spoke. "True. I haven't even looked at the accident report yet. I don't think I've ever looked at it. It's…too hard, and each time I picked it up, I started to bawl, so I just put it away and…well, I refused to think about it. That goes for the newspaper article, and the obituary the Billings paper ran. My pastor cut them both out for me, but I haven't read them yet. I thought this place was on the other highway."

Zane accepted his coffee. "It was an honest mistake, considering your condition."

"I was pretty upset by the time I got down here. The police officer bought me a cup of hot tea. And…" She pulled in a breath as she zeroed in on a far wall. "And we had to turn around here. I couldn't see the crash site. I was too… Anyway, the police were so good to me. After the officer bought me the tea, we just returned home." She looked at the waiter. "Do you know where the crash site is?"

"Sure. It's at the end of Lindbergh Lake Road, or close to it. I can draw you a map, if you like. The last turn is terrible, but they've never done anything about it, not even after the crash. Costs too much money to put up a simple sign, I guess." He pulled out his order pad and sketched out a map on the back of one sheet, explaining to them exactly how to get there.

Unable to stare at it for too long, she blinked and looked around, carefully assessing the seating area.

"You know," the waiter said gently when he returned, "I talked to your folks just before the crash. The police even asked me a bunch of questions."

Wide-eyed, Kristin asked, "What did you say?"

"I said that your folks seemed fine. They said they were on their way to visit a friend."

Kristin knew of no friend down here. She bit her lip. No one had been able to figure out why they were down this way. Not only had the reason for the crash remained a mystery, but also the reason for the trip. "Did they say where this person lived?"

"Nearby, I think. There aren't too many people who live year-round on the lake. I'm really sorry your folks died. They'd been in here before a few times and were really nice."

They were here before? Her heart rate hitched up slightly, but with that short remark, he moved away to greet a trio who'd walked in. Still frowning, Kristin watched the well-dressed blond man hold the door open for a slim, African-American woman. Behind them, a rugged-looking man with a tough expression entered. They ignored Kristin and Zane as they found a table at the other end.

"Mom and Dad didn't go anywhere without telling me

where they were going," she told Zane, glad they were alone again. "But this time, all they said was they were doing 'church stuff,' whatever that means now."

"Had they said that before?"

"Sure. Mom and Dad visited shut-ins all the time."

"They could have been visiting a fellow parishioner."

"Down this far? No one from our church is from outside Westbrook."

"Maybe the person moved away before you could remember and they were keeping in touch with him. You'll have to ask your pastor for sure."

"You're probably right. Besides, this has nothing to do with our trip. It just had me thinking. And it looks like it's just another unanswered question. Like the dead end you got with your search for your brother."

Kristin watched his jaw harden as he looked away. He didn't want to get hurt again with another dead end. Sympathy tightened in her throat.

He deserves his brother, she thought, surprising herself with the desire to see Zane happy. He didn't want to be alone any more than she did. But they could both end up that way, she realized with an ache in her chest.

Lord in Heaven, help us. Have us find both my mother and his brother. Only You can do this.

Oblivious to her thoughts, Zane went on, "We should tell Jackson about those two men at the Mexican restaurant. If they are capos or soldiers in the Martino family, they'd be known to McGraw." He looked at her. "Are you okay?"

She snapped out of her short prayer. "I was praying. What's a capo?"

"It's a rank in the Italian Mafia," he said quietly. "A capo is a man in charge of a gang or a crew. They are well respected, but often the men under them are anxious to be known, or be 'made,' as well. What it boils down to is that there's always someone looking for promotion and respect, and killing you would achieve that. It's also possible they've been ordered to kill you. We have to tell McGraw."

"He's coming here in a couple of days." She looked around the restaurant, accidentally meeting the eyes of the young woman who'd recently entered. Instantly, she shifted her gaze away, wondering if the woman actually knew they are talking about murder, Mafias and things like that. She finished off her coffee. "Let's get going. We shouldn't be here wasting time."

She slid off the seat, pulling out her purse to pay for her coffee. Before she could manage that, Zane had already set some bills down. Wordlessly, he led her out of the restaurant.

The trip into Missoula was quiet. Kristin couldn't help but look at the Mission Mountains to their right, and at that one peak, Sheep's Head.

The mountains that had been her home for so many years had new meaning. Death, missing people, searches. All of a sudden, she wanted to stop Zane, tell him to take her home, and forget about everything.

No. She'd given up seeing her parents' accident site and reading the report. She wasn't going to give up her search to know her birth mother better.

They finally made it into Missoula just as Kristin's stomach began to growl for some belated lunch. She ignored it, focusing on finding the police station, and subsequent nearby coffee shop Clay had suggested.

A few minutes later, they were parked along a wide street near the café, and close to the meandering river that cut through the city. The trees had not yet filled out, but several cyclists were speeding past Zane's car.

Inside, Kristin spotted Clay West immediately. To her surprise, Violet Kramer sat beside him. He stood for them, shaking Kristin's hand and introducing himself to Zane, before introducing Violet.

Kristin peered curiously at the woman. With thick dark curls, obvious femininity and high heels, Violet looked everything Kristin wasn't. But the woman smiled warmly, her eyes surprisingly sympathetic as she offered her condolences for Kristin's loss. Thankfully, the incident this morning wasn't mentioned.

"I asked Violet to come," Clay said as they sat down at the small table. "I hope you don't mind."

Violet leaned forward. "I'd have invited myself, anyway."

"I don't mind," Kristin answered. "I've read all your articles since that story on that girl, Gwyn. It was good how she really tried to redeem herself."

"Her story had to be told. It's sad that she died." Violet studied Kristin carefully. "Clay found an old article about your father in the Billings newspaper. In fact, when Clay and I went down to Billings, we stopped by your family's old church. Reverend Taylor was still there."

Kristin nodded. "He came to see me after my parents died, with a copy of the article you mentioned. It showed an old photo of us." She paused, feeling sheepish. "I didn't read the article, I'm afraid."

"You look just like your mom looked when I knew her," Clay said.

"Thank you for seeing us on such short notice," Zane said after ordering two coffees from the passing waitress. Giving in to her stress, Kristin added a blueberry muffin.

Clay continued. "I don't know where Eloise is, though. Jackson asked me the same question, but I couldn't help him."

Kristin listened carefully. Was that how Clay knew Jackson?

"Why don't you tell us what you *do* remember about Eloise? How far along in her pregnancy was she?" Zane asked.

He thought a moment. "I think she was starting to show. Once she'd said to me that she got involved with someone she should have left alone."

"Did you ever meet him?" Zane asked.

He shook his head. "Not that I can remember."

Zane took his coffee when it arrived and set it down in front of him. "Was there anything about Eloise that stood out?"

"She loved to bake. Oh, she could bake up a storm with just about any fruit the home was given. Once, we'd been given some huckleberries and she made pies with them."

Kristin wrinkled her nose. "I find the seeds too hard," she said.

"I didn't care. They barely touched the sides going down when I ate them. Eloise really did like baking. She wasn't allowed to make any meals, but she was allowed to bake stuff for the younger kids." Clay let out a reflective laugh.

"Did she ever talk about where she'd like to live some-day?" Zane asked. "A favorite spot, or what she'd like to do for a living?"

Clay set down his cup. "No, but she was anxious to have her baby and was the kind of woman who was determined to succeed, no matter what happened to her."

Eating her muffin, Kristin knew what Zane was aiming for. His subtle questions, while probably noticed by Clay, were forming a picture of a woman that neither of them knew in great detail.

After draining his coffee, Zane set down the empty mug. "Anything more?"

Clay shook his head. "Eloise handled her pregnancy with dignity. She was just that kind of woman." They talked for a few minutes before he looked at his watch. "I'm sorry. We have another appointment we can't get out of."

"Wedding planner," Violet explained. "It's the only time we can both spare."

After smiling at his fiancée, Clay stood and turned to Kristin. "I'm sorry I'm not much help. Ever since you called, I've been racking my brain for something to help you, but it was a long time ago. She was just a nice girl who loved to bake."

Violet rose, too, and smoothed down her tailored outfit. "Kristin, if Jackson warned you not to try to find your mother, you should really do as he says. He's only thinking of your safety. These people are dangerous people."

She glanced at Clay. "Let Jackson do his job. Then everything will work out."

"I wish I was that optimistic," Kristin answered.

Clay shrugged on his jacket. "One other thing. She wasn't ashamed of your father. She just said he was the wrong person for her. I know now that she witnessed a Mafia hit, and was involved for a short time with the Mafia, but back then, I didn't know anything. Eloise always told me to keep strong. When she left, I missed her. It's because of her that I became a police officer."

The engaged couple said their goodbyes and left. Kristin fished through her purse for a tissue. Clay's words were sinking in, and already those foolish tears were starting again. She had to toughen up.

"Let's go," Zane said gruffly. "I need to get back to my office."

"Did Clay say something important?"

"Maybe. It sounds like Eloise might be forced to start her own business. If she applied to work for someone, she'd be concerned that she'd have to reveal her past in a résumé, but if she worked for herself, she wouldn't have to answer questions about who she was."

Kristin nodded. "That's a good point, but remember it takes money to start your own business, and credentials to borrow money to set up a business."

"True. I'll know more after I do some research. I set up my own business here, so I know the ropes, and even how to get around them if you don't want to give your social security number."

"Is that even possible?"

"If you know certain things to do, yes."

As they climbed back into Zane's car, Kristin asked, "Do you think she'd start something that has to do with baking? I mean, she wasn't trained in anything else and I checked most colleges. I used every name I could think of that would be similar to Eloise Hill, but nothing came of it."

"She could have been baking just to relieve stress. Still, she'd need money. Do you know how many bakeries there are in Montana?"

"I have no idea."

"Nor do I. I know it's a long shot, but worth looking into. Plus I want to know what your parents were doing down here. I can't help but wonder if it were related somehow to your mother. They kept all that info on her, and they were interested in helping people less fortunate." With that, he started driving.

Could that be? Could her parents have had some contact with Eloise? Kristin found herself smiling. The day *was* a success. She'd met someone who knew her mother, and that small connection encouraged her. She would find her mother. She would be able to move past the sadness of losing her parents and onto the joy of finally meeting her birth mother.

She turned to Zane as he made their way out of the valley in which Missoula was situated. "Clay did know more than he realized. How do you know the right questions to ask? Was that in your training?"

"Nope. Private investigator training is broad and deals mostly with privacy laws, how to do surveillance, and people's rights and such. But I have learned a few other things over the years."

"Like what?"

"Like never drive a van."

She frowned. "Why not?"

"Because most P.I.s drive vans, and that makes people suspicious. And never drink *anything* while on surveillance."

She laughed, far more relaxed with Zane than she ever was before. It felt good to be there with him. With a short glance over at him, she found her heart hitching slightly at his clean, angular profile. She liked being with him. A lot.

The Mission Mountains came back into view. The smile that had lingered on her face faded. Was she starting to care for him? Was she ready to set aside her grief and hurt to see if she could move on with her life?

Zane could search for bakeries when they got back, but right now she needed to put one more thing behind her.

She turned to him. "Zane, I want to visit the crash site. I'm ready now."

NINE

"Are you sure?"

Kristin blew out a long, calming breath. "Yes. I know it takes time away from your search, but a few hours aren't going to change anything."

"But a few hours can mean the world if your life is in danger. We need to keep you safe."

"And if someone is after me, would they think that today of all days, I'd decide to see where my parents died?"

"You were headed here, so maybe they *would* think that." Zane grimaced. "We could argue this all day, Kristin. I'm only thinking of your safety."

His words warmed her. She felt her face heat, and something lodge in her throat. "I appreciate this. But, Zane, we're down here and I'm not alone. It won't take much out of our day, will it?"

She watched Zane glance at the car's clock. It was late in the afternoon. Finally, he nodded. "As long as you think you're ready for it. But it may be harder than you realize."

"You've seen me cry at the drop of a hat. I have been grieving for months. My birth mother was an orphan. She lived in a foster home. Clay lost his parents, too. They both rose above it, and they were younger than I am now. I need to do the same, and I need to be as strong as my mother was. I'm ready to deal with my adoptive parents' death. I have to do this before I deal properly with finding my mother."

He nodded. Did he understand the way she felt? Had he already dealt with the grief in his life and risen above it? Kristin scooped up the hand-drawn map she'd tossed onto the dash after they'd left the rest stop and tilted her head to study it. "It says we have to drive down Lindbergh Lake Road until we see the lake in the distance." She looked up and blew out a noisy sigh.

"Having second thoughts?"

She snapped her head over. "No! I mean, I don't want to be afraid to come here. And unless I face this now, I might never face this. It could become almost a superstition, not wanting to come here, and avoiding this place to keep myself safe. I don't want to think like that."

He lifted his eyebrows. "That's pretty deep."

"And that surprises you? Do I look like I don't think deeply?"

She watched as his neck then his face reddened. "I didn't mean it to come out that way. I was just commenting on the fact that it is a pretty deep thought, as though you might have considered it before."

"Not this particular thing, but similar ones. In the weeks after my parents died, I didn't even want to get groceries for fear of running into someone who would say how sorry they were. Before long, I wasn't going to places that I associated with my parents."

"What's changed your mind?"

They were coming up on the turnoff to Lindbergh Lake. The narrow lake sat oddly broadside in the long valley. She glanced around them. "Seeing others rise above it. People like Clay and my mother, and even that woman Violet wrote about. I remember my pastor saying that avoiding things will only make them harder to deal with. He said things could become a superstition and they would begin to take over a person's life, and I didn't want that."

"I forced you out of all that?" As he talked, he turned onto Lindbergh Lake Road.

"Yes, you did. But that's good. I needed to be forced." She stretched out her hand and laid it on his warm forearm. Under the lightweight jacket, she could feel his muscles. They were very tense.

Of course, he'd be on edge. Someone was after her, and she'd dragged him into it. And it wasn't fair for her to have done that.

She pulled back her arm and stared out the front windshield, hoping to catch sight of the lake soon. She was pretty sure she was going to cry when they got there, but for Zane's sake, she hoped it was all over quickly. He'd already had to deal with her tears several times this week.

She stole a quick glance at him. He was frowning, deep in thought. What was he thinking about? His brother? Or maybe defying Jackson's express order to stop her search? Was he thinking that the search could get them both killed, as Violet had inferred?

She shivered despite the comfortable temperature in the car.

"There!" He lit up and pointed.

Kristin leaned forward. "I missed it. Was it the lake?"

"Yup. See?"

She'd expected them to look down on the lake, but rather, as the road bent, they caught the smallest glimpse of the shimmering waters in front of the dark, sheer face of the Mission Mountains. There was hardly any descent toward the water.

She read the directions again. "We have to go to the left and follow the lake until we see a signpost that's bent over."

Tensely, they followed the map in silence for several long minutes, eventually seeing the small signpost the waiter had mentioned. The only thing keeping it upright was an arrow-straight pine acting as a splint. The sign showed the symbol of a look-off.

This was the place where her parents had died.

Zane pulled off the road, almost brushing the trees on her side. He noticed her curious look at pulling over on a lonely stretch of semi-dirt road. "I noticed another car behind us, so I don't want to block it when it goes by. Are you ready?"

With a nod, she threw open the door, then waded through the bushes, all the while carefully containing the swelling feelings within her.

Please, Lord, just be with me. I need strength.

Zane was pointing to the break in the trees. "I can see where the car veered off the road. Look at the damaged trees."

Whatever tow truck or crane had been used to fish the car from the water had also cleared out a narrow swathe of trees. Yet, there remained evidence of a small look-off at the end of the damage. Chewed-up pieces of a wooden viewing station had been bulldozed to one side, leaving only a small portion of the platform behind.

For a few minutes, Kristin stared down at the cold, dark water. Spring always raised the levels of lakes and streams, and now the water lapped against the rocks and trees and chunks of the battered station, threatening to rise farther still with the melting mountain snows streaming into the cold, dark lake. Erosion had eaten away at the shoreline, drawing it closer to the road than perhaps the first travelers had planned.

She shut her eyes. She still had no idea why her parents had come down this narrow, lonely road. There was nothing but cottages here and only the past few days had it been nice enough to entice their owners to open them for the summer.

"Why would my parents come here in January?" She wasn't really asking Zane, who stood quietly behind her. The question just slipped out.

"There must have been a reason," he said. "We should have asked the waiter. He seemed to know a lot. Do you remember who reported the accident? It's not as though this place sees a lot of people."

She shook her head. "The police probably told me, but it didn't sink in. It would be on the police report in Dad's filing cabinet, I'm sure." She swallowed. "Maybe I'll read it someday."

He stepped forward, peering down at her. "Are you sure you're all right?"

She nodded, even offered a small, calm smile. Somehow, she could hold back the desperate loneliness within her. She actually *did* feel more at peace. Was it because of Zane's presence?

She drew in a deep breath of cool, lake air. "I'm fine. Really, I am. It's hard to explain, but I'm okay with being here. I feel a strange kind of peace."

Would Zane understand that? From what he'd said, he didn't believe in much anymore. She smiled up at him. "I do feel better. I'm glad I came. It's sad, and I will probably feel it when I get home, because my house is so empty now. But right this minute, it's okay."

With that, she turned to walk past him, ready to leave here knowing that her mom and dad were together in heaven.

As she passed close to him, Zane reached out to touch her hand, and suddenly, she didn't just want him to rub her arm, or pat it as he might a neighbor who'd lost her precious cat.

She wanted more. She turned with him, and boldly wrapped her arms around him, hoping to soothe not only her own pain, but also the hurt someone had caused him.

He accepted her hug with his own. And as she held him, she wondered at her sudden brashness. She didn't go around embracing people, except those few older ladies at church who were only too glad to offer hugs and advice and help with her loss.

Regardless, she laid her head against his chest, listening to his steady, strong heartbeat and wondering if she should be praying for wisdom in dealing with him, instead of praying for peace.

He set her away from him and tilted his head as he looked at her. "Thank you."

She smiled. "I kind of figured you needed a hug as much as I did."

"Well, a guy would have to be nuts to turn down a hug from a beautiful woman." His expression became uncomfortable for a moment. "As we came down this road, I actually prayed that you'd feel better."

"You did?" She bit her lip, afraid to say something that might embarrass him, or push him further from God.

He shrugged. "It worked. God answered it. I prayed you'd find peace here."

She swallowed. "God is good. And life with Him isn't about condemnation, Zane. It's about love. God loves us."

He stared at her for a moment, studying her eyes in great

detail, it seemed to her. She thought she saw a glimmering tear there, but wasn't sure. It might have just been a reflection of the brilliant sun or the white peaks of the Mission Mountains.

"Forget everything you've been taught about God," she added softly, "and just let Him teach you what He wants you to know. Ask for wisdom and you'll get it."

"Have you?"

Turning, she peered around him at the glimmering water. "I think I have. It's as if God is taking a bad situation and bringing something good out of it. I don't know what that is yet, but I think it may include you," she said, feeling self-conscious at sounding as if she was falling in love with him.

It couldn't be that. They'd only known each other for a few days. Hardly enough, and yet being with him was suddenly extremely important to her.

He lifted those dark brows of his. "Maybe so. I have to admit to being mad at God for such a long time that I've hardly been listening. It was as if God had so many rules for me—"

"Zane!" Interrupting him, Kristin spun him around to face the watery vista through the trees. The steep climb of green mountains at the far side of the lake was reflected in water, albeit in a wobbly, shimmering way thanks to the stiff breeze. "Recognize this?"

"It's Lindbergh Lake, Kristin."

"It's more than the lake. I see McDonald Peak and Sheep's Head Peak, and I think…" She spun around, scanning the roll of land behind where they stood. "This is incredible! This is the exact spot!"

What was she talking about? Zane watched her nonetheless scramble up the short embankment opposite the lake, then hurriedly cross it to peer up at the gentle slope on the other side.

"There's something up there."

He squinted at the side of the hill. "It looks like some kind of a shelter."

"It's a small cabin. It looks like it's on a rocky ledge up there. I bet that's where your brother stayed while he painted this view. In all the seasons."

"Who?"

"Bobby Kendall. Don't you recognize this site?"

"From the painting at the university? I didn't see it, remember?"

"Sorry. You're right. But I saw it, and I'm sure this is the spot. Bobby could own that cabin up there and come back to it! Any time!"

Zane shook his head. Not today.

But he found himself smiling at her attempt at private investigating, despite the fact that she and her mother were in danger. "I'm not going to stake out this place if that's what you're suggesting. Your safety is too important."

She looked a bit sheepish, then picked her way back down the short hillside.

"I guess you're right. But I traveled all the way through New England after the trial with no problem, so I figured it would be okay to stand out here in the middle of no-where. I know I have to be careful, but remember I wouldn't be hard to find if someone really wanted to locate me."

Zane frowned, hating that she was right. "Didn't Violet mention something about a newspaper article and an old photo of your adoptive parents and you? If Clay could find it and see the resemblance to your mother, what's stopping the Mob from doing the same?"

Nothing would, he realized, suddenly not liking the quiet world around them. The breeze had died, and only the sounds of nature broke the silence.

It was too quiet here.

He cocked his head to one side, listening. Over the gentle music of nature, he could hear the low growl of an engine. Someone back a way was idling their car, someone beyond the last slight bend in the road.

The car behind them should have passed them by now.

And they hadn't passed a cottage in the past half mile of this old dirt road, so there was no reason to be sitting back there, idling. Whoever had been following them had now stopped, as if knowing they were stopped, too.

Still up the side of the hill a few feet, Kristin looked down at him. "You're acting like you've tuned me out completely, you know. I was talking to you."

"Get down here. Now!" His words were cool, brisk and meant to grab her attention.

She obeyed, scurrying and sliding down the hill to him. "What's the matter? What do you see?"

"I heard a car revving its engine. I think it's the one behind us that I was expecting to pass by here. We didn't pass any cottages where they could have stopped. Someone knows we've stopped and is waiting for us."

"Just up past the bend, you mean? How would they know we'd stopped?"

"I was wondering the same thing." He twisted around to stare at his car. A car tracker? Those devices were as small as a cell phone and could easily be attached to his car when he wasn't around. Whoever was idling their car up the road a bit could be tracking them. How else would they know that he'd stopped?

He strode over to the side and began to search the wheel

wells and bumpers, but found nothing. Gritting his teeth, he muttered, "Get in."

"Where are we going?"

He didn't answer. Instead, he started the engine, shoved the stick into Drive and eased onto the dirt road.

"Isn't this road a dead end?" Kristin asked.

"Yes. But we're being followed."

"How is heading toward a dead end going to solve anything?"

"I don't know if it will. Put your seat belt on. And you may want to pray."

"As long as you're praying, too."

"I plan to." *God, I was a fool to head down this dead-end road when I knew someone was after Kristin. Now I'm going to need Your help.*

He listened to her pray, a low, barely audible prayer as he picked up speed. Sure enough, they came to the end. A narrow driveway wound into the dense evergreens. There was a cottage or house beyond, but he wasn't planning to endanger whoever may be there. They may have even known Kristin's parents, because what other reason would the couple be down this way in the middle of winter, but to see whoever lived here?

The reason eluded him. He needed to get back to his office to find that out. In the meantime, there were more pressing issues.

At the last driveway, he slammed to a stop and backed around. Dust and gravel peppered his wheel wells.

Kristin gripped the dashboard. "What are you doing?"

He pulled along the edge of the rounded end of the road, partially hidden by the trees.

"Are we going to just sit and wait for them? This road isn't wide enough for both of us."

"I know, but hopefully they'll stick to the right as they reach the end of this road. That should give me enough space to whip past them and escape. They'd have to turn around. I don't think that driver plans to race past us with guns blazing. Not on a dead-end road."

"Who's to say he's not going to do it anyway?"

"He wants a show. He and whoever's with him. They aren't here to rid themselves quietly of an informant, then dump the body into the lake, never to be discovered. These guys have been biding their time while we were stopped to make sure they get plenty of mileage out of killing you."

"That's a whole lot of assumptions. What if they fire at our windshield?"

He tightened his grip on the steering wheel as he stared at the potholes left over from the winter. "Not the easiest thing to do on a bad road like this, when you have to lean out of your side window and take aim."

"Oh, so they won't fire at us. They'll ram us instead!"

Zane said nothing, focusing his thoughts on how to get Kristin out of this unscathed.

They idled there at the end of the driveway for several long, painful minutes. Very quiet minutes, they were.

Nothing happened.

Zane worked his jaw for another minute. Still nothing. Finally, he eased forward.

"What are you doing?" Kristin whispered.

"I can't hear the car anymore. I was expecting them to follow us down here."

"Do you think they gave up?"

"I'm hoping so. I need to get you out of here, immediately."

He maneuvered a gentle curve at as fast a speed as he dared to go. The way, though flanked by tall, arrow-thin evergreens, was now straight, but only for a short time. There was another gentle curve before they returned to the crash site. Zane felt sweat bead on his brow.

The way straightened again; the crash site came into view. Suddenly, from around the next turn, a dark blue car roared.

A tall, heavyset man was driving, while another man hunkered down in the passenger seat. Zane watched as the driver yanked hard on the steering wheel. The other car careened into the center of the road, toward him.

These guys were trying to run them off the road! "Get down, Kristin!"

Automatically, he veered to his right, but when the thick branches scraped against the window, he glanced around. If he shifted any closer to the right, they would crash into the dark woods. But to steer to the left meant they'd crash into the other car or, worse, plunge into the icy lake.

The other car matched his move.

"That guy wants to run us off the road!" Kristin called out.

Zane reached over and shoved her head down.

He didn't want the last thing she saw on this earth to be where her parents lost their lives.

TEN

Zane stiffened. Kristin might trust God with her life, but was he willing to face his Maker, too?

Lord, this is it. I've been mad at You for too long. If You care, then save Kristin.

Please? I want to trust You. I want to love You like Kristin loves You. I want her peace.

Between the two cars lay the place where Kristin's parents had died. The break in the trees caused by the accident was clearly visible.

His foot felt glued to the gas pedal, his hands sealed to the wheel. He couldn't move even if he wanted to.

Beside him, Kristin lifted her head, but he couldn't shove her back down. He couldn't move a muscle.

She cried out something as they raced toward the oncoming car. Somehow, they ended up in the center of the road.

They were so close. Zane's shoulders stiffened further.

The two men were swarthy, angry and obviously arguing. He could see the passenger grab the steering wheel. They were the ones from the Mexican restaurant.

Zane cut hard to the right, anything to avoid the dark plunge of lake that had killed the Perrys.

But the other driver didn't react fast enough, or maybe the passenger's own grip on the steering wheel was too hard. Whatever it was, at the last minute, they swerved, hard and fast to their right, and in that instance, their car hit a bump, flew over the embankment, over the remains of the look-off station, and down, down toward the lake.

There was a sickening thud. One tall tree that had survived through the winter unscathed now quivered and shook.

Then there was a huge splash.

After racing past, Zane slammed on the brakes. Kristin had wedged herself against the dash with elbows locked, but she was already twisted about, staring over Zane's shoulder at the wreck site.

"They went into the water!"

Slamming to a stop, Zane shoved the shifter into Park. "Call McGraw, Kristin. Tell him someone just tried to kill us, and they're in the lake." He disconnected his seat belt.

"Are you going in after them?"

"I can't let them die, as much as they wanted to kill us."

Her eyes like watery dinner plates, she bit her lip. Pausing, he slid his hand around her neck to pull her close. "It's okay. Everything will be fine."

"They tried to force *us* into the water. How did they end up there?"

"I think the passenger grabbed the wheel."

"We could have died, too!"

"We didn't." On an impulse, he leaned forward and pressed his lips against hers.

She was soft and warm, and he could feel her hiccup as she tried to keep her fear in check. He pulled away. "Make that call, okay? And then open the trunk. I have dry clothes in there. And there's a gun under the passenger seat. Get it out."

He pushed open the driver's door and alit. Wasting no time, he peeled off his jacket and sweater and kicked off his shoes as he hurried down the embankment.

The frigid water stole his breath the second he dove in. He followed the bubbles from a spot several yards out that showed where the car had sunk. He dove down, and he found a door handle. Fighting his own restricting clothing and tightly held breath, he tugged hard on the driver's door. The pressure of the water kept the door closed. Clamping down on his jaw, he wedged his knee along the car frame and tried one more time before he needed to return to the surface for more air.

Lord Jesus, I've given You my life again. Give me a couple more seconds.

Zane stared into the car. It was filling fast with water. The passenger window was open, and the two men were beginning to panic. They needed to equalize the pressure inside and act before the door would open. Only a few more moments.

The door relented, and gave in to his next hard tug. The last air bubble ripped past him on its journey to the surface.

Zane followed it up for a breath, and then dove down again. The driver had already released his seat belt, and kicked himself to the surface. Zane let him, then reached in to release the passenger's seat belt. He managed to click it free.

His lungs screaming for air, he pushed himself backward and then shot up to the surface again. Breaking free of the water, he sucked in air and coughed. Beside him, a moment later, the second man broke free of the water.

"Get out!"

Zane blinked up at the shore. Kristin stood on one large rock, her face knotted with determination, and both hands on a gun that she pointed at the water.

His gun, which she'd managed to find pretty quick. He only wished she wouldn't point it at him with her finger on the trigger.

"I said, get out of the water! Both of you!"

On either side of him, the men began to swim to shore. He swam with them, reaching the shore first before pulling himself easily up onto the broken remains of the look-off. He saw that Kristin had removed his dry clothes and dropped them at the edge of the road.

The men climbed onto the look-off station beside him, both heavyset men in poor shape and wheezing desperately from their unexpected dip. One fell down, and with a hard shove, Zane helped the other to the wooden platform.

He was freezing, and about to shake violently, but before that, he grabbed the driver's collar. "What were you doing?" he demanded. "Who are you?"

The man began a coughing fit as he lay prone on the wood. The other man twisted around to see if Kristin still held the gun, but Zane flipped him back by pressing his knee onto the man's upper spine. "I asked you a question!"

"You're not going to get away with trying to kill us, you know!" the guy snapped back with a wet cough. "We'll get you!"

"I just saved your sorry hides. Now, who do you work for?"

Flexing about, the man swung his fist at him wildly. Zane answered the man with a short punch, which sent the man facedown on the weather-beaten wood.

He looked up at Kristin. "Did you call McGraw?"

She nodded. "He said he'll take care of the men. If you can get them secured somewhere, he'll send out someone to apprehend them. He sounded like he could make it happen immediately."

"Good." He glanced up the side of the hill across the embankment to the road. The cabin wasn't that far up, and both men were still conscious enough to climb up there. He jumped across to the road. She turned to him, gun and all.

He pushed gently on her hand so the weapon faced the two men wheezing on the platform. "I appreciate you helping with that, but be careful. It's loaded and has no safety."

"Oops, sorry. I found it after I called Jackson. Zane, you scared the death out of me jumping in that water! You could have been killed!"

"And these guys definitely would have been if I hadn't tried."

"Well, don't do it again, okay? Here are your clothes. You should get out of those wet ones."

He scooped them up. "They aren't for me. These two will have to share them."

Turning, gun and all, she gaped at him. "You're going to let them go?"

Again he moved her to point the gun at the men. Then, reconsidering, he took the firearm from her. "No. I'm going to tie them up in that little cabin up there, after they get out of their wet clothes, that is. Jackson can find them there. In the trunk are some electrical tie-downs. They look like long pieces of white plastic. I'll use them for handcuffs. Go up to that cabin and see if it's unlocked."

She nodded and, after finding the ties for him, she went to check the cabin. He pointed the gun at the men. "Get onto the road. You two are going for a little climb."

The men struggled to make it to the road. They were shivering and running out of energy fast. By that time, Kristin had already reached the cabin and had slipped inside. A moment later, she returned to the doorway and called down to him. "It's empty, but there's a bench that you can tie these guys to. I think they'll be okay here for a while."

"Good. Come on down and get into the car."

She skittered down the short distance to the road. With the gun and holding the clothes and the tie-downs, he ordered the men up the way she'd come. Still wheezing, the two men climbed up ahead of him. Both looked beaten, crushed and freezing cold.

Once the trio was inside the small cabin, he ordered them to change into whatever dry clothing he had. He was taller and slimmer than both men were, and he doubted the clothes would fit either man properly, but they'd die of hypothermia if they remained wet. Once they were squeezed into his changes of clothes—a pair of old jeans, sweatpants, a T-shirt and a sweater—Zane ordered the shorter, weaker-looking man to tie the taller man to the bench leg.

That done, he then knocked the weaker man down to the floor where he quickly tied up that man beside his buddy, and then secured one leg of each man to the other with the remaining tie-down.

"Last chance to talk," he told the taller man.

"Forget it. You're a dead man."

"Gracious as always, I expect. Who do you work for? Martino? Which one?"

"The old guy. He'll be really proud of us when we're finished with your girlfriend, pal. Then, he'll die in peace knowing the woman who ruined his life is dead, too."

Ahh, he thought. The old don was dying. That explained plenty. But more important, the guy had just explained something even more crucial. These guys were mistaking Kristin for her mother.

Improbable, but hey, they'd seen Kristin only from a distance, and even Clay had commented on how much she looked like her mother, even that old photo of her in the Billings newspaper she'd mentioned.

Back to Billings again. But he needed time to figure that out, something he didn't have right now. "A tribute killing for Salvatore Martino?" He shook his head. "Look around you, buddy. You're in no position to be threatening us at all. I'm beginning to regret pulling you morons out of the water."

"Then you're the moron for doing that," the bigger, more belligerent one slurred back. They looked like fools, sitting on the floor, hands tied behind their backs, half-dressed in ill-fitting, dry clothes, their own in two wet heaps beside Zane. The shorter one was barely conscious, and sported a split eyebrow. "We have friends, and once we get your girlfriend and her daughter, we'll be back for you. No one messes with the Martinos."

"Tell me where Martino is." Short of telling them he had Kristin Perry, not Eloise, standing down by the road, he didn't know how to ask about their evidence.

Neither man answered. The cabin was dimming as the sun had begun its descent behind the mountains. The only window in the place, a small, filthy thing at the back of the cabin, faced east into the dark woods. He wished he knew more about the whole Martino case. He could use it to question these idiots, get the truth from them, instead of listening to their blowhard boasts.

Forget it, Zane told himself. These two weren't planning to talk, and frankly, if they belonged to the Martino Mob, they would rather die than talk, because talking usually meant dying, anyway.

Tearing two strips from one of the men's wet shirts, he

gagged them both, just in case they found the lungs to call out and the person who lived down here was curious or foolish enough to find and release them.

That done, he shoved his gun into the back of his jeans' waistband and walked out. The few steps down from the tiny building onto a grassy ledge were battered, and his foot indented a weak stair tread. He yanked off the teetering banister and jammed it through the old-fashioned door handle. At one end, he rammed the whole narrow board between the loose trim and the plank siding. He shoved the other end into the doorjamb. Even if they got free and tried to open the door, it would take some hard pulling to break the board.

He hurried down the hill to Kristin. She climbed out of the car, and watched him shrug on his jacket and shoes.

"Give me your cell phone," he finally said.

Wordlessly, she handed it to him. He checked the number she'd dialed and hit redial. After a minute, he got Jackson McGraw. He told the deep-voiced man where to find the pair he'd fished out of the lake, taking the opportunity to quote their exact coordinates from the GPS in his car.

"And," he added, feeling the irritation of nearly allowing Kristin to be killed, "if and when you get here, we need to talk. Because I'm taking personal offense to the FBI telling Kristin about her mother then not allowing her to find the woman. And then not doing enough to keep her safe while Vincent Martino's boys are looking to satisfy a deathbed wish to get some idiotic glory."

"Zane Black, right?" Jackson gritted out. "We'll be talking, but I can assure you that I consider Kristin's safety to be my top priority. I have a team in the area and they'll be at your location within minutes. Until I can get there, you had better keep her safe, or I will go after you myself."

The chest thumping done with, Zane hung up and handed the phone back to Kristin. She snatched it and shoved it into her jacket pocket. Her eyes were watering and her chin wrinkled with barely contained emotion. "How could you do this?"

"Do what?"

She shoved him hard and only because he wasn't expecting it, did he move at all. "You know what I mean! Risk your life by diving in there to save those two men! Then you just tie them up in that hut and expect me to calmly let you call Jackson as if we've found some piddly lead in some stupid case! You think that you can say one prayer to the Lord you've been shunning for years and then can suddenly be so cavalier with your life?"

He caught her wrists as she tried once more to shove him, and pinned them down at her sides. "I trusted God. Isn't that what you wanted?"

"I want to wait on the Lord!"

"Well, I don't, and I don't think He wants us to wait, either. That's a cop-out, an excuse, and I took a chance that God wanted me to do something in faith first!"

She yanked back her arms. "I suppose you prayed down there in the water, too?"

"I did." Suddenly, he found himself annoyed by her question. "And you know what? I gave my life back to Him, fully expecting Him to take it, even though I asked Him not to. But He spared it. And you know what else? God may want us to wait sometimes, but He wasn't waiting for me. He's been after me for years. Only after I met you, did I realize that He's been planning my life, forcing me to notice Him!" He dropped his voice and pulled her close, knowing he needed to calm them both down.

He took a deep breath and relaxed. "I'm sorry if this

all has to take place where your parents were killed. It must be hard."

She softened and shook her head. "Actually, no, it's not. To be honest, seeing this place was easier than I thought it would be. Nevertheless, to know that those men were saved, when my father and mother weren't, that's hard. And the thought that you nearly died, too."

He released her. Of course she'd heard him yelling at Jackson. "I'm sorry. And I just found out from those goons that they think you are Eloise."

"But Jackson thought that they were after me personally."

"They still are, according to those guys. But these guys think you're Eloise. It's hard to believe that they would make that kind of mistake, unless they are getting desperate. But Salvatore is dying, and they may only have a few days. So they're trying to kill both of you as soon as possible."

With a shaky sigh, she wiped her eyes and added, "Did they say anything else to you?"

"Nothing worth repeating."

"And you just let them sit up there out of the wind, in dry clothes while you're freezing to death here?"

"Kristin," he whispered against the wind as he caught her arm. In truth, he was very cold and turning numb. "I'm sorry. I wanted facts from those morons. I had no idea how my actions would affect you."

She lowered her head. With one finger, one of them that still ached from hitting that guy in the cabin, and was now stiff with cold, he lifted her chin, and then, feeling his heart pound inside him, he hauled her in closer.

And kissed her.

She gripped him back, holding him tightly as he pressed

his lips hard against hers. She was warm, and though he knew he was probably chilling her to the bone, it felt so wonderful to hold her and to feel how much she cared for him after so many years of not having anyone who cared about him.

But he had a brother out there. A family of his own. And she needed to find her own family. Once she found hers, she'd be gone maybe into hiding again, and who knew where his search would take him? They were just passing through each other's lives.

Hating how that painful thought cut into his kiss, he gently set her away from him. She swept her hair from where it dropped into her eyes, and looked everywhere but at him. "Jackson said he was going to send some people to pick these guys up. He said they were in the area."

"He said something similar to me, too. In that case, I don't want those two in the cabin to get another look at you when they bring him out, so we should get out of here before they come. Did Jackson say why his associates were in the area?"

"No. But it sounded like they are really close." She peeked up the hill at the cabin again. "Will those guys be all right?"

"They'll be fine. I, however, am freezing."

"I imagine. I'm freezing and you just got the front of me wet. Let's go back to that rest stop for a coffee."

Zane would rather not stop there, but he needed a hot drink and a change of clothes immediately. He'd begun to shiver hard and was in danger of losing precious body heat. The rest stop sold sweat suits and T-shirts in its tiny gift shop. Maybe he'd find something in his size.

Quickly, they climbed into the car and drove off. Less than half an hour later, he pulled out onto the highway. As he turned left, he saw a large, nondescript silver car approach Lindbergh Lake Road.

Through the windshield, Zane recognized the occupants from those who had stopped at the rest stop. Beside the blond driver was the black woman also seen at the restaurant. The tinted windows wouldn't allow him a view of the backseat, but Zane bet that other man was with them, too.

He kept going, not saying anything to Kristin. Those three would have to be Jackson's associates. Why were they here? If it was to keep an eye on Kristin, he'd say they were doing a poor job of it. But they were FBI, so they wouldn't be slackers. Were they here just to look for Eloise?

He wasn't going to get his answers right now. Not with the rest stop coming into view. No one was there except that waiter wiping tables in the brightly lit seating area. Zane was glad for the privacy.

The waiter gaped at Zane as he walked in. "What happened to you?" He hurried behind the counter and quickly set two mugs onto the counter, then filled them with hot coffee.

"I took a quick dip," Zane muttered. Though he'd warmed up slightly in the car, he felt chilled to the bone. Kristin walked straight to the small gift shop and found a sweat suit for him.

After purchasing it with soggy bills and then quickly donning it in the restroom, Zane accepted the waiter's offer of a plastic bag in which to put his wet clothes.

The waiter washed the counter where lake water had dripped onto it. "This doesn't have anything to do with that car crashing into the lake just now, does it?"

Kristin's head shot up. She'd been quiet, staring darkly

into her coffee mug. "How do you know about that already?"

"The old guy who lives nearby called me. He asked if whoever had driven into the lake had stopped by here first. He wanted to know if they'd said anything about why they were there."

"What did you say?"

"I said several cars had stopped here. Two men and a woman, when you were here, then later, two other guys pulled in, each grabbed a coffee to go and left. I have to tell you, they looked like pretty unsavory characters. I think one of them stole one of the fundraising chocolate bars I have by the cash."

"Wait a minute," Zane interrupted, setting down his mug. "*Who* called you?"

"Joey Hamilton. He lives on the lake. Says he saw most of what happened through the woods at the edge of the lake."

"There's a driveway at the very end of the road," Kristin asked. "Is that where he lives?"

"Yup. He's a bit of a recluse, and doesn't like strangers, so he keeps a watchful eye out for them nowadays." With his fingertips, the waiter tapped his temple in that knowing way.

Kristin looked at Zane as he sipped his coffee appreciatively. He used both his hands to hold the mug.

"Maybe my parents were going down to visit him?" she asked him quietly. "To take some things to him, perhaps?"

The waiter shook his head and answered for Zane. "I don't think so. He has a son in Missoula who owns a bakery and grocery store and once a week brings him whatever he asks for."

Kristin exchanged a glance with Zane. He could feel her

energy rise. A bakery? Did that have anything to do with her parents? Or her mother? If her mother was such a good baker, would she have worked there? Zane didn't believe in coincidences, and yet this seemed to be a genuine one.

But why go down to this old guy's place anyway? Were her parents friends with him, as they'd told the waiter? A mentally ill recluse didn't seem the kind of friends Kristin's parents had. Perhaps he'd been a client of her father's once.

The waiter refilled their mugs, and offered more cream and sugar. "I see your car didn't get dunked in the lake, so it must have been the other one. So why did you jump in?"

Before Kristin could quite innocently answer with the absolute truth, something he didn't want her to do, Zane spoke. "That's not important. What is, though, is that the lake is one cold body of water."

The waiter laughed. "Dead right on that. With the snow-melt being later than usual this year, I'd say the lake will stay cold all the way to August. Those police divers are going to find it chilly, too."

"Police divers?" Kristin echoed.

"Sure. I called the police. Joey Hamilton won't call. Like I said, he doesn't care much for visitors. So I called them. They should be racing past soon. Was anyone hurt? Did you fish those guys out then just leave them on the road?"

Instinct kicked in, hard and hurriedly. From his wet wallet, Zane dug out some more dripping bills and after paying for the coffee, he grabbed the bag of wet clothes. "Those guys will be okay, but we have to get home. It's been a long day and I need a hot shower."

Kristin caught his fast glance and slipped off her stool. "Thank you for everything. We're sorry we have to rush off, but don't worry about those two men. Though, tell me about this Joey Hamilton's son. Do you know the name of his grocery store?"

"It's Hamilton's Home Bakery. The grocery store part is small, but the bakery is very popular." He frowned at them. "You're not in any trouble, are you?"

She smiled at him as she followed Zane to the door. "No. But if you kept our presence here to yourself, we'd appreciate it." She hastily added, "We don't want you to lie, of course, but we'd rather no one know we were here."

The waiter looked suspicious. "I can't promise anything."

She looked sympathetically at him. "I understand. Thank you for everything."

"Are you sure you're both okay?"

She smiled at Zane, then at the waiter. "Yes, thank you. It's just that, quite frankly, the less people know about us, the better it is for us. We're not running from the law or anything. Quite the opposite, really. We're just—"

Before Kristin unabashedly told the man her whole life story, Zane stepped in front of her. "Look," he told the waiter. "All we're trying to do is keep a low profile. We're not fugitives, but for our own safety, we have to avoid everyone. I realize that you don't know us from Adam, but it would mean a lot to us if you kept quiet about our visit."

The waiter looked at Kristin, then Zane, and then slowly nodded. Obviously relieved, Kristin headed out the door, but she stopped just as Zane held it open. He'd rather she just walk out and stop this chitchat, but to make a scene and yank her out might provoke the waiter to say something to the police.

Jackson had told Kristin not to trust the police even, and after discovering that someone had removed the grease stain from her vest, Zane wasn't about to trust them, either.

As if sensing Zane's feelings, she walked out. A moment later, they climbed back into his car and drove north again. At one point, several minutes later, an ambulance shot past them. A few minutes after that, a police cruiser, lights blazing, ripped by.

Kristin shot him a wide-eyed glance.

They weren't stopped.

And Zane thanked God privately for that small mercy.

ELEVEN

All the way home, Kristin's thoughts were a jumble of fear and worry. She'd said more than one silent prayer for her and Zane's safety, and that the FBI would apprehend those men. And that wisdom would prevail.

But she'd also wondered repeatedly about the bakery in Missoula and its rather odd, almost tenuous connection to her parents. Of course, that was assuming that her parents were on their way to visit it, via Joey Hamilton, that fateful day.

But to find out for sure, she'd have to wait until she got home to dig through her father's files. He had been meticulous about record keeping.

She'd tried once to read his files, shortly after the safe had been opened, but the memories attached to anything of his had been too raw.

Not so now.

"I'd like to go home, if I can," Kristin said quietly. The request was the first thing she'd said since leaving the rest stop. "Dad would have written something down about this trip, I'm sure of it. If it was for the church, he'd do it for the pastor. If it was work-related, he'd need it for the office's records. If he'd been searching for my mother, then he'd make sure he kept notes on that."

Now, as he took the only exit into Westbrook, he nodded. "I'd like to do some searches of my own, too. First up, I want to know who in the Martino crime family knows how to make a bomb. And I hope you're right. There must be something that would explain your parents' relationship to Joey Hamilton."

"My parents never mentioned him. Dad kept meticulous records, not just in his work, but with his personal stuff, as well, all in separate files. But he didn't talk about work much. There's going to be a lot of files to sort through. He'd been on staff at the church, too, so he kept receipts for that."

"What did he do at the church?"

"He handled all their legal issues, of course, but he also assisted in pastoral visits. The pastor liked to take someone with him. Mom would go, too, especially if they were visiting a widow. Dad would keep records of all the visits."

"Joey Hamilton's house seems a long way to go."

"True. And the pastor always went with them. I'm sure Joey Hamilton wasn't a part of our church. I've never heard of him before now. We'll search my father's office." She nodded, wet her lips and tossed him a quick look. "Um, I'm sorry if I talked too much back at the rest stop. I hope I didn't say anything unwise."

"Don't worry about it. I have a feeling that that waiter isn't going to say too much about us." He threw her a smile. "And I appreciate your honesty."

She tried to smile back, but the memory of those men, racing toward them, trying to force them to their deaths…it was too strong.

They passed familiar houses on their way to her home, Kristin feeling the heat blasting from the vents. Although very warm now, she couldn't turn the fan down. Zane must still be cold. "We ended up with more questions than answers today, despite meeting Clay. I'm beginning to realize why Jackson asked us not to look for my mother. And yet, on a totally unrelated drive, we nearly get killed."

"I'll get you home safe and sound where you can figure out what your parents were doing down there."

"But what about Hamilton's Home Bakery? Don't you find that just a little coincidental?"

"Kristin," he began as he pulled into her driveway. The motion sensing light came on in the approaching dusk. "Do you have any idea how many bakeries there are in Montana, especially if they are part of grocery stores? People have to eat, and it could just be a coincidence that your mother liked to bake. Lots of teen girls like to tinker in the kitchen."

She nodded. He was right, of course, but still, as Zane said, she knew that real coincidences were rare.

They climbed out of the car. Automatically, he dropped to his knees and peered underneath it. "It's got to be here. I didn't have a good enough look before—" He reached farther and yanked out a small box about the size of a cell phone. "Here it is."

After straightening, he removed the battery. "There, no more spying."

They hurried into her house. "I'll wash your wet clothes," she said, taking the heavy plastic bag. "Maybe they'll be dry by the time we're done."

She then indicated to him to follow her into her father's office. There, she handed Zane a folder that her father had entitled "church stuff" from where it lay on her father's desk. He may as well search while she filled the washer.

Kristin worked mindlessly for the next few minutes, then after preparing a small snack for them—stress always made her hungry—she returned to her father's office.

When she entered the warm, bright room, she stopped. Zane sat in her father's chair, behind the broad, dark desk. Having always loved this room with its bright sunny corner windows and warm, dark furniture, she used to sneak in when her father was working. The only thing now marring the pleasant memory was the gaping hole in the far wall. She'd have to call that drywaller soon. "I really like this room, you know. Always have. My dad used to let me lie on the floor in front of the fireplace and color in my coloring books while he worked. Though, I used to chatter on a lot, so I don't know how much work he got done."

"Maybe he could tune you out?"

"Probably. It's not as though I said anything deep and important. Mostly silly stories about the pages I was coloring, I think." She cleared her throat as she set down the snack on the desk's polished hardwood surface. Enough of the sad memories. She had a lifetime ahead to reminisce.

By herself, maybe? She stole a furtive glance at Zane, his dark head tilted down as he opened the folder.

Forget it. Forget about what she and Zane shared back there at Lindbergh Lake. They were just releasing some extra emotion. A kiss meant nothing nowadays.

To most people, that is, she told herself.

They pored over the surprisingly thick file. She took the gas receipts and a map and carefully compared the two. With a set of colored markers, she marked the stops her parents had made on various trips.

Zane took the other receipts plus a variety of papers, then watched her at her task. "It looks like they went down to Missoula often," he said when she finished. "I've compared dates and times. They'd go to Hamilton's Home Bakery straight from here, and then on the way back, stop at the rest stop some time later. But what's a bit confusing is the place is north of the turn off to Lindbergh Lake. They'd have to backtrack if they were going to visit Joey Hamilton."

"It's just a few minutes north," she countered. "There are no gas receipts for Missoula, so maybe my father got into the habit of going there for gas before heading down to Lindbergh Lake. Plus my mother probably wanted to stretch her legs. She would get cramps in them. Is there anything useful in the other receipts?"

"No, and they rarely purchased groceries in Missoula, so I have no idea why they went there in the first place. There's one receipt from Hamilton's Home Bakery, a loaf of cheese bread and a block of old cheddar. From Christmastime last year."

"I remember that. They gave both to our minister. It's odd, though, to drive all the way down to Missoula for cheese and bread. Our deli downtown has both. And even I can make a decent cheese bread." She fell silent immediately.

The quiet echoed around them. Was Zane thinking what she was thinking? That her parents had found her mother in that bakery? Did she dare to call with the hope her mother worked there? What would Jackson say should he find out?

"There's a phone number on the receipt," Zane noted quietly, "but it's too late to call now. We can call tomorrow."

She sagged in her chair near the wide desk. "I guess. I wonder if the people who work for Jackson got to those men before the police did."

"Probably. The police arrived after the FBI and they'd be told that the FBI was in charge, and would have to back off."

"Because those two men are wanted for attempted murder?"

"No, because it would be part of a federal case, the case against Vincent Martino."

"I hope those two wise up and tell the FBI the truth. But they didn't seem the kind to start blabbing. I hope the FBI actually finds them. I doubt those two would call for help."

"Especially considering the fact that I gagged them."

Despite herself, Kristin giggled. Zane's deadpan expression struck her as funny. Maybe it was the whole incredible situation, like nothing she'd ever experienced before, which made his remark seem something light and funny.

"How do you know that Jackson's men got there before the police? I mean, we passed that police car about ten minutes after we left the rest stop."

"I saw a car pull onto Lindbergh Lake Road just after we pulled out. Plus, remember Jackson knew you wanted to talk to Clay West."

"Yes!" She lit up. "Do you think he'd sent someone to follow us?"

He shrugged. "He may have suspected you were looking for your mother, and decided to get an agent or two closer to you. That would explain how they managed to get to Lindbergh Lake so quickly. But they could also be searching for Martino or your mother."

Again, she thought of what that waiter had said about Hamilton's Home Bakery. Was the Lord leading them there?

Her heart revved at the thought she could be talking to her mother tomorrow. How was she ever going to sleep tonight?

Tension built in her, and she reached for the last snack

on the plate. But stopped. She'd be as big as a house if she continued to eat when she was stressed. "I should get out and exercise. Go for a walk or something."

"Not just yet. And you shouldn't be leaving your house whenever you please." He softened. "I know it's hard to sit and wait. I've been doing that for a couple of years because my own search for my brother had to be put on the back burner so many times. But trust me on this. I've seen a lot more garbage than you have, and it's better for you to just stay here."

She pursed her lips. "I've seen my share of tough stuff, too, especially dealing with the aftermath of my parents' deaths."

"What do you mean?"

"All I could think was that my family's lives were suddenly reduced to a few paragraphs in various obituaries. And only one short article about Dad in the Billings paper. At the time, it struck me as garbage. Great, Godly lives, but who cares? That's all my father got after all he'd done for Westbrook and Billings." She paused. "I sound ungrateful, and un-Christian. Forget I said that. I was hurting back then."

He lifted his head. "I remember reading about their deaths. It made news all over Montana."

She shrugged. "Dad's law firm had done some prominent work in Billings years before I was born. The newspapers called him the 'Billings Bonanza.' When he relocated up here, he got the nickname the 'Westbrook Whiz.' Dad was good at his job. He used to get calls from people in Billings asking him to move back there. Years ago, for a human-interest story, the newspaper in Billings ran the article about Mom and Dad, and the work Dad did, with a picture of the family. When I went to the Marshal's Office in Billings with that note from my mother to Jackson, a few people from there offered their condolences. At the time, I thought they deserved more. I was hurting so much."

"That must be how the Mafia learned of you. While you were doing your chores just now, I called a friend in Chicago. He said that there was no way that the Mafia could get a hold of the list of who was allowed in the courtroom. And if you weren't followed, the only other way would be that article and the family photo and the obituary."

She thought a moment. "There wasn't even a warning about the road my parents were on being dangerous. It kind of hurt. Like they died for nothing."

Zane could feel her pain, though just as he was to comment on it, she interrupted his thoughts. "Zane, I know it's dangerous, but there must be something I can do besides cower here reading my father's notes. Things like finding out who owns the cabin where you put the men. It could belong to your brother."

"Then he'll end up there this summer, and we'll have a few months to find him. I have a few other feelers out, Kristin, so never mind my search for my brother."

He pursed his lips. Kristin had no idea how hard it was going to be to find a person who'd been hiding successfully for twenty years.

For all they knew, Eloise was dead.

"I should go," Zane said quietly, hating the possibilities rifling through his mind. "You need to rest, and I need a shower, plus do a little digging into Joey Hamilton's life. Not to mention who might know how to build a bomb. I know the police will be looking into that, but I plan to help them."

"Don't do anything unsafe."

He studied her in the warm light of the office. As she'd said, it was a nice room. The colors here suited her. "As in jumping into a lake? Don't worry, most of my searches are from my desk." He found the corners of his mouth tilting up.

Her lips parted, and for the first time ever, his breath caught in his throat. He couldn't pull away from the intensity of her gaze.

They were getting involved. It was as if their lives were tightly entangled somehow. Was God offering this woman to him? Was she to be his family, because they would never find her mother or his brother?

Did he even want a family? he asked himself. He hadn't exactly had a great one growing up. And he probably wouldn't be very good at handling one now.

He rose, too tired to analyze his thoughts anymore. When she followed him to the door, he said, "Lock up everything, okay? Keep your cell phone handy and turned on. If anything happens, call me, okay?"

She nodded. Those rich green eyes shimmered, not from unshed tears, but from a depth he hadn't noticed before. She smiled, ever so slightly, her smooth lips bonded together, keeping her smile in firm check.

She was beautiful. So beautiful.

As she reached for the doorknob, before his courage drained away, he dragged her closer to him.

Their third kiss. She returned it, shyly, he thought. She acted as if she didn't know what to do.

And yet it felt good to hold her, to have her kiss him back. To feel needed and loved and wanted and cared for. Was this what love was? He stopped kissing her, but still kept her close, feeling her uneven breathing on his neck.

Finally, he let her go, walked out the door and closed it firmly behind him.

He heard her lock it, and watched from the edge of the driveway as she returned to her father's office. Once there, she closed the curtains.

An hour passed before Kristin moved from her father's desk where she'd been reading his files. As she was stretching, the phone rang.

It was Zane. "I've got something of interest for you. You remember that other P.I. I had looking for my brother? I asked him to check out Joey Hamilton. It turns out that Joey's a retired investigator."

"Really? Maybe he'd worked for my father at some point, and Dad asked him to do one last search?"

"My thinking exactly. He's been checking out a woman named Tammy Lockhart in Missoula. She's thirty-nine, with brown hair and green eyes, and works as a cook in a small retirement home outside of Missoula." He paused. "It's not uncommon for lawyers to use investigators in their work. It could be unrelated to your search. But I have her address."

"Wait." After sitting down, she'd quickly perused one file her father had marked "private." She found a small notation at the last line.

The name Tammy and an address, in her father's short, choppy scrawl. She read aloud the address.

"It's the same," Zane said.

Her heart pounded. Her father knew of this woman? Had her parents been headed down to Missoula that fateful day to meet her?

Or were they on their way back from it, and having found success, decided to drive to Joey Hamilton's place to pay their bill?

Excitedly, she asked, "When can we go?"

"In the morning, if you're up for another long drive to Missoula."

"It's not that far." Yes, oh, yes, she was ready to go. That Tammy Lockhart could be her mother.

"Then I'll pick you up at eight. We'll get an early start." He hung up.

Still sitting at her father's desk holding the phone, she dialed Jackson McGraw's number. She wanted to tell him about Tammy, to ask him if he got those men, but at the last digit, she stopped and hung up.

What would he say to her? To stay put, that was what. He'd do the checking, and who was to say he wouldn't take this woman into protective custody again? To a safe house, where Kristin would never see her?

And yet, there was a small part of her that wanted him to. A part of her wanted to give up, if only to keep everyone safe where they were and to assume Martino's men would give up.

No, she couldn't take the risk. Martino had found her mother at the last safe house. Giving up on her search was no safer than hiding Eloise away.

Though, Jackson was only thinking of their safety. Was that because Jackson was her father, and not this Danny Douglas? Zane's speculation had put a small suspicion in her own mind.

Did she even dare to believe she had a father out there? That the name on her birth registry was written to keep Jackson safe? That Jackson wouldn't tell to protect her mother?

Closing the file, she turned to the cabinet. Then turned back to the desk, frowning. When they'd first come home, she'd found this file on the desk, and handed it to Zane.

But hadn't she put it away a few days ago? Nothing else was out of place, and she'd had several files out at that time, preparing herself for her first meeting with Zane. But she'd always returned the files to the cabinet. This office was always kept neat. Her father liked organization. Her mother had been neat to a fault. Her own room Kristin kept clean. A place for everything, and everything in its place.

Would she have left this file out?

She'd always loved this room for its neatness. It defined her father and she'd made a point to keep it like that, even after his death.

Did that mean someone else had left this file out?

Had someone been in her house since she was last here?

TWELVE

Doubt rolled over and over in her mind. She lay awake for hours, listening to every sound, analyzing each noise and wondering if she should call the police, or Zane, or panic or pray.

She prayed. Zane had been tired when he left, and all she had was an uncertain feeling. Jackson was in Chicago, and Kristin did know one thing for certain. She didn't want people traipsing through her house. And finally, she drifted off to sleep, only to awaken too early and drag herself into her bathroom to prepare for the day. She told herself that since she was safe, she'd only imagined the file had been moved.

Downstairs, she went through her usual morning routine of making coffee and toast, as she'd done by herself for the past few months, missing her parents and their small talk, their quirky morning habits and the routine they'd followed for years.

Pushing aside the melancholy, Kristin lifted her head. A car was pulling into the driveway. She checked the clock on the microwave. Almost eight.

But Zane's arrival changed her thoughts, and the cold wash of danger chilled her. She should have called Zane with her doubts, even if he would have insist she go to a hotel. What had she been thinking?

She'd been thinking how her life would be out of her control again.

"Good morning," she said as brightly as she could manage when she opened the door for Zane a moment later. "What's that you have?"

He hefted a bag from the coffee shop where they'd first met. Kristin saw that his knuckles were not as swollen as yesterday after he'd subdued that thug. "Pastries, and in this hand," he said, lifting an envelope in his other hand, "the report from the lab. I picked it up on my way here. You can read it while I drive."

They climbed into his car, where he said, "Open the lab report first. See what it says."

She tore open the flap and, after pulling free the paper-work, she scanned it, zeroing in on the bold print at the bottom. Zane leaned over.

"Graphite paint, as I suspected," he said.

She looked up, finding him a bit too close. And yet she liked having him close. She cleared her throat. "Paint?"

He didn't seem bothered by being so near. "I figured it was that. Why is that a surprise?"

"It's only a surprise that you suspected it. But it doesn't really narrow it down for us. Westbrook U has an art department."

Zane's expression hardened. "True. But do you know what a black mark means?"

"No."

He took the report. "The Mafia uses that symbol to tell people it's a Mafia hit. At its most basic level, the black on a dead person's hand can mean that the victim hadn't cooperated with the Mafia."

He returned to his reading. "It says here that this particular sample has the same chemical composition of a unique brand of paint that's made only in Chicago." Zane fell quiet as he read. Finally, he spoke, and his words cracked slightly. "There's a short blurb on the paint. It's used for its luminous gray quality on grisaille. I don't know what that is, though."

"That's a monochromatic painting."

Zane drilled a stare into her. "Like that Kendall one at the university?"

"It's not monochromatic, but it used a lot of similar color tones." She bit her lip. "Come to think of it, it does have a shimmering quality to it." She frowned at his closed expression. "The paint must be used by half the art department. I'm not sure it would mean anything. Surely the Mafia doesn't use this specific paint."

"They don't necessarily. It's just odd that it's used here, while at the same time, the Mafia is after you."

"Then I'm glad you're helping me."

He smiled at her. "Maybe the Lord is giving us what we need instead of what we want."

A family, she thought. *Are we slowly becoming a family?* Shyly, she turned away, to take a shaky bite from one of the pastries he set on the dash.

Are we not to get what we hoped for?

Zane seemed oblivious to her desperate thoughts. "On the way to Missoula yesterday, you said your mother had already been in the Witness Protection Program. Do you think she could have returned to it without Jackson knowing?"

"I don't think so. His brother, Micah, in Billings, was the person I first contacted and he directed me to Jackson. But he would have said something to him, and there would be no reason for him to lie to me. He would just tell me that she's safe in the program." She bit her lip. "Do you

think that she's already been found and killed, and someone is hiding the truth?"

"That almost suggests a cover-up within the Marshals."
Zane frowned at his own words. "And if that was true, then
why would the Martino family be after you?"

Kristin bit her lip. He softened, and squeezed her hand
before backing out of the driveway. "I'm sorry. I should have
kept my mouth shut. Especially after the day you had yesterday. Did you find anything useful in your father's office?"

She thought of the files she'd found open on father's
desk. Should she tell Zane what she suspected? He'd want
to protect her. He'd insist she return to the hotel, away from
home, the house that was filled at the same time with
painful and yet comforting memories.

Maybe she did leave the file out. It wasn't as if she'd
been on the ball these past few days.

Quickly, she threw a glance over at Zane before tucking
away the pastries. If she didn't set them far from her, she'd
eat the lot of them.

They'd reached the highway and were cruising along it
before he spoke again. "I am beginning to read you like a
book, Kristin. Something's bothering you."

She sighed, giving in. Convincing him there was nothing wrong seemed to demand more energy than she had.
"Well," she began, "I noticed that the file I gave you had
been on the desk. I thought I had put it in the filing cabinet
before I met you, that's all. I'm not sure, though."

"Do you think someone broke in and read the file?"

"I don't know."

"You have a burglar alarm, right?"

"Yes, and it was set. There was no sign of a break-in.
I'm probably wrong. Forget I said anything."

"No, I won't. I will, though, check out that alarm when

we get home." He tightened his jaw. "You should have called me."

She nodded. And it scared her just how much she regretted not calling him.

The file incident bugged Zane. He didn't like unexplained incidents. Sure, considering all that had happened, Kristin could be mistaken, but not when he weighed the facts of her getting pushed into traffic, the two thugs following her, or even those same thugs taking a dunk into the lake. And the most notorious Mafia family in recent history was after her.

Zane had spent most of last night doing serious research into what Joey Hamilton had been investigating. His P.I. friend had felt badly enough about the dead end on his brother to help him out, and together, after several long phone calls, they'd discovered who Joey had tried to investigate back in January.

Tammy Lockhart lived and worked in Missoula, and fit the general description of Eloise Hill. And she cooked for a living.

He yawned. He hadn't had time to call Jackson McGraw, though he'd planned to. He wanted to know everything about that pair he'd fished out of the lake. But considering that the local police hadn't yet contacted him, it meant that the waiter from the rest stop hadn't told the police anything, and for now, he'd take that as a gift and keep quiet, even where the FBI was concerned.

They ripped past that rest stop, with Zane feeling relieved that Kristin didn't ask to stop there. They tore past the turnoff to the lake and still she stayed quiet. Small mercies, but he'd take them.

Missoula greeted them just after noon. Zane had a good idea where Tammy Lockhart lived and found her small suburban house without any trouble. They pulled into the driveway and parked behind a Honda Civic. He'd already learned that the woman had the day off.

As they got out, a large dog bounded over to them, his tail wagging and his bark loud and insistent. Without waiting for a pat, he raced to the front door and jumped up, his nails scratching the panels. It was obvious from the scratched-up paint that he'd been doing that for hours.

"Looks like he wants in," Kristin murmured. "She must not be home."

"Whose car is that, then?"

Kristin shrugged, stepped up to the door and rang the bell. The dog barked again, for the moment allowing her to pat his head.

Still no one came to the door.

Leaning past her, Zane turned the doorknob. The lock clicked easily and the door opened a crack. The dog nosed his way in and disappeared into the cold, dark house.

"Ms. Lockhart?" he called out. "Are you there? We've let your dog inside."

As if to answer, the dog barked in the back room, then whined loudly. Then barked again. Cold dread washed over Zane as he stepped over the threshold. An odd smell drifted into his nostrils, a bit acrid and metallic, and he knew what it was.

"Stay here," he said.

Kristin gripped the doorjamb. "Why? Do you think something's wrong?"

He didn't answer. Instead, he stole carefully down the dim hall, following the dog's pitiful whines. In the cool, back kitchen nook, he found what he suspected.

Tammy Lockhart was lying on the floor, two gunshot wounds in her chest.

THIRTEEN

"Didn't I tell you to go home and give up this search?" Clay growled at Kristin as they stood just outside the front door.

Zane stepped between them, glaring nose to nose at the police officer, who'd been the first to respond, probably because he'd heard Zane Black's name.

"This isn't her fault, West," Zane snapped back. "I did the search for this woman last night based on what Joey Hamilton had found out back in January. Obviously, someone else did the same research that Joey Hamilton did."

Clay pulled a face. "Joey Hamilton? You both should have known better, especially with that old nutcase."

Kristin squeezed between the two men. "A woman is dead, so both of you stop throwing the blame around here." With her palms on their chests, she physically separated them. "Look, Clay, as far as I knew it, the two men Zane fished out of the lake were the only two after me or Eloise. And we still don't know if the Mafia did this or not. Your coroner refused to confirm the time of death, and you have no other proof." She drew in a breath. "For all we know, a jealous boyfriend could have done this."

"You should have taken Jackson's advice and given up

your search. Vincent Martino has escaped custody and is most likely here searching for you or your mother."

Both Zane and Kristin frowned. Kristin spoke first. "Jackson told me that he believed Vincent was here looking for me. But how would you know that? For that matter, why is Jackson telling you all this?"

"I can't answer those questions. But every law enforcement office in the country is on the lookout for Vincent. And we know that Salvatore is close to death. It's logical the son is going to do everything he can to avenge his father, preferably before he dies, so he can tell him about it."

"And the only way you could know that for sure is by talking to Jackson." She sighed. "Look, I don't care if you've been talking to the president about this, but I decided that my search for my mother can't be any riskier than her being in that safe house all those years ago. I was nearly killed back then."

She stiffened her spine. "And I have yet to see Vincent Martino here. He'd be a fool to come here with Montana crawling with law enforcement officers, federal or otherwise."

Zane listened to her tirade, expecting Clay to acquiesce, but then remembered the dynamic reporter that the police officer had recently proposed to. Clay would have to be tough.

"This situation is of your own making, Kristin," Clay answered. "You have led someone here to Montana. How else would they know to go after Tammy, a person your father had been ready to contact? You told me just a few minutes ago that you think someone broke in to your home and read your father's file."

"Someone *may* have broken in to my home. And I didn't

lead anyone to Montana *or* here. We don't have all the facts yet."

"How else would the shooter get this woman's address, if not from your father's files?"

Kristin swallowed. Zane knew Clay's words affected her deeply. And judging from her glance down the hall, she was wondering if that was her mother there. His heart squeezed in sympathy.

She shook her head. "If the Martino family found out I was in Montana, then it was from someone else who knew where I was. Like maybe from that article in the Billings newspaper."

Zane watched Clay West's expression change ever so slightly. Kristin's words had hit a nerve. No, maybe not a nerve, but something the police officer knew, or suspected. Was there a leak somewhere in the system? Was someone feeding the Martino family information? Someone who knew Kristin? A cop gone bad or someone who worked with the FBI or the Marshals?

"The Mob knows Eloise is somewhere in the state, and hadn't bothered with Kristin until they decided to flush Eloise out." Zane hated to voice his concern, but he had to face the facts. Ignoring the situation, as his mother had done for so many years, wouldn't solve anything. And they needed the truth about Tammy Lockhart.

Clay's expression turned skeptical. "That's assuming Eloise knows where her daughter is, though."

Kristin looked back down the hallway, where that woman, Tammy, lay on the floor. From this vantage point, they could only see the sheet-draped feet. Zane heard her small gasp.

"Kristin?" he asked.

She looked back at him. "So this woman wasn't my mother?"

Zane turned to Clay West. The man shook his head, as his voice dropped. "No. I spoke to Micah McGraw a few minutes ago. Tammy Lockhart was really Tamela Longpré. She'd been in the program for about five years, having been a mistress for an arms dealer down in Texas before that. The guy died in prison eighteen months ago, but Tamela decided to stay here with her new identity." He looked at Kristin. "I'm sorry. She wasn't your mother. Joey Hamilton was wrong about her."

As devastating as that was to Kristin, Zane felt it necessary to add, "We know that the two men who have been following Kristin think she's Eloise, and don't know that she's the daughter."

Clay nodded. "I know that the Martino family has been targeting women who are younger than Eloise, because it's hard to guess an age sometimes. But that doesn't mean that someone in the family won't realize who you really are. That photo with the article in the Billings paper might just be all someone else needs to find you. Either way, you're in danger."

A man walked in from the where the poor woman's body lay. With gloved hands, he held out a small clear square. "I've lifted a smudge from the floor. I believe it came from the woman's hand. It's some kind of black grease."

"May I see it?" Zane asked.

The man showed him the square, and Zane studied the way the light hit it. Kristin leaned in close, too. "It's not grease, but graphite paint," she said. "And it's made only in Chicago."

Zane added, "You can check with the lab at Westbrook U. They tested something similar that had been on my car seat."

"Explain," Clay asked.

Zane told Clay about Kristin's vest, and how the smudge was transferred to his car seat. Then about how the smudge had been removed from the vest before it could be tested. Clay took some notes, then as he finished, he touched Kristin's arm to move the three of them away from the entrance to the house.

At the front door, Zane looked down toward the kitchen just as the coroner's staff wheeled the body into the hall-way. He could feel Kristin stiffen as she witnessed the poor woman's last trip from her house.

Time to get Kristin home, Zane decided. They should-n't be here anymore. They'd already given their state-ments, and hashed and rehashed the merits of coming down here. Zane refused to allow Clay to blame Kristin, though she'd done a good job of standing up for herself.

They left the house. A neighbor stood at the end of the driveway, holding the dog by the collar while talking to the police officer who'd moved Zane's car—the second one, as his other one was still parked at the hotel—from the driveway to make room for the morgue's vehicle.

Zane steered Kristin away from the pair, and toward his car, where another officer had parked it.

As they drove away, they passed Violet Kramer speed-ing to get to the scene. Zane blew out a sigh. He'd already learned that the ambitious reporter had been looking for her big break, that one great story to put her into the big leagues. Well, he didn't want Kristin interviewed and put back into the spotlight again.

Heading back to Westbrook, listening to the silence lin-gering between them, Zane was tempted to turn on the radio.

Finally, Kristin spoke. "Maybe I *should* stop searching. Maybe it is *me* who caused this needless death."

"It's not, Kristin. This woman died before we got here. She could have been dead a week for all we know."

"You don't believe that, do you?"

"Why not? It's been pretty cool this May. Her back window was open, her heat was off, so the house never warmed up. I don't know anything more, but I do know you're not to blame."

"They're starting to kill women because of me."

"No, they aren't!"

"So who is killing them? And what's the connecting factor here?"

"A leak in the system, that's what. Someone believes the women in the Witness Protection Program, the ones they're killing, are your mother, and they know about you. They didn't follow you from Chicago or Maine. They learned of you from someone in the FBI or Marshal's Office or who lives in Billings."

"How do you figure that?"

"Someone saw you at the trial, or someone read that article in the Billings newspaper, and told them. Though the article is online, not many would know where to find it. But if you subscribed to the paper, you'd have seen it. And who else would subscribe, but a local person in Billings?"

"The only people who knew who I was were Jackson McGraw and his brother, Micah. I really don't think they'd be feeding the Mob information."

"I agree, but you're not to blame, either."

"I just think if I hadn't started my search, then that poor woman on that stretcher would still be alive. You remember what Violet said about how dangerous this is. She said she was pretty shaken up herself by her own investigation. What we need to do is—"

"What we need to do is get you home, check your alarm

system, update it if necessary and get back to work reading your father's files. We can't solve the leak problem, and we can't change that Joey Hamilton got the wrong woman, and we can't change that whoever broke in to your home got it all wrong, too. But we can find out for sure what your father had discovered."

"I wonder why Mom and Dad had been looking for Eloise."

"You say your adoptive parents were not young. Maybe they felt they needed to find your mother in case something happened to them. Given what you've told me about your dad, he wouldn't have given up his search unless he was convinced he'd found your mother."

"He was good at his job."

"And you have a similar bulldog attitude. I'd say it was from watching your father work all those years, while you were coloring in his office."

She smiled. "Maybe I have learned a few things from him."

The rest of the trip home was quiet, with Kristin actually nodding off to sleep for part of the journey. When they arrived back at her house, dusk was falling fast. The first thing Zane did when they let themselves into the house was to check all the door locks and windows.

Then he checked the burglar alarm. "How old is this thing?"

"It's not the most up-to-date, but it works just fine. I did set it last night. When I came down this morning, I did what I always do, hit the deactivate button. If I don't, I'll accidentally walk out and set it off."

"That's good, but this system is easy to bypass."

She hugged herself, and Zane knew she was doing her best to hold back contrition.

He set his jaw. They both needed to be tough right now. "We're going to change the locks on all your doors, and upgrade your burglar alarm system. This is the basic model that probably suited your family for years, but it's obsolete."

She nodded. "The insurance company had suggested that when my parents died. Jake, the one who cracked my safe, can do all the upgrades. He's licensed to upgrade this system, he told me when he first came here. He must have noticed how outdated it was."

"We'll call him. Do you think he can come first thing tomorrow?"

She suppressed a yawn. "Maybe. He's a good friend."

Her words proved true. Jake was there early the next morning, and together with Zane's help, he replaced all the locks and upgraded her system, adding a sensor by each door.

Thankfully, her parents had set in place the ability to upgrade should they choose to and she did have the financial means to do it. Zane and Jake worked diligently all day, until finally, just after five, Jake announced that they were done.

He spent the next half an hour explaining what he'd done and how the upgrades worked. Then, after declining the offer of supper because he was due at his sister Maggie's apartment for a meal, he left.

Kristin set about making their own hot supper while Zane reviewed her father's file, and made a few phone calls from the office. The large map her father had often used covered the dining-room table and Zane had been consulting it regularly. Afraid she'd lose the various small notes and receipts, she carefully placed them back into the file and returned it to the office before she set the table. The meal ready, they sat down in the dining room and Kristin said grace.

"I saw your father's map and his markings on it," Zane said when she finished.

Leaning over to help herself to the vegetables, she looked at him. "Anything unusual?"

"He's marked Missoula, Billings and Lindbergh Lake a lot, but there were some notes scribbled on the edges."

"He used this map with his work, so I wouldn't—"

Abruptly, the sharp crash of breaking glass interrupted her, followed by the burglar alarm ringing out, piercingly loud. A thump sounded in the kitchen.

Zane jumped up. "Someone's trying to break in!"

"Break back in, you mean! He's come back to get more info!"

"The alarm company will call 911, and—"

The phone rang, and Kristin hurried out of the dining room. As she reached the hall, Zane yanked her back.

Just in time, too. A loud crack, the report of a gun, ripped through the noisy air above the alarm's piercing wail.

"Stay back!" Zane pulled her farther into the dining room before tearing across the hall to her bedroom. Back against the wall, he pulled a gun from his waistband.

Gun raised, he tore into the kitchen.

The phone continued to ring, and Kristin raced out of the dining room and into the office to answer it, knowing it would be her alarm system's monitoring office calling to check on her.

But more important, she needed to grab the file. No matter what happened, she didn't want her father's papers to fall into the wrong hands. One woman had already died because of that.

Her hand clamped down on the file, but as she scooped it up, its contents spilled out, including the papers and bills they hadn't yet studied. Most papers slid over the edge of the desk and fluttered to the floor.

With a flustered mutter, she looked down at the phone then the papers. Behind her, the sounds of crashing and thumping broke up the insistent ringing.

She stared at the door, frozen in indecision. Was Zane all right?

The ringing continued. Finally, ignoring the file's contents, she reached for the phone. "Hello?"

"Ms. Perry? This is your security company. We have an alarm sounding in your house. Is everything all right?"

"No! Something's happening!" She hated how she was panicking, but Zane was out there, maybe even dead on the floor.

"It's all right. We're notifying the police. Where are you in the house right now? Are you alone?"

The alarm shut off, drenching the house in cold silence. Leaning over the desk, Kristen gripped the phone tighter. "No," she whispered. "My friend is in the dining room. I'm in the office. And someone else is out there."

"Is there a door to the outside in your office?"

"No. I'm trapped in here." She slid down onto the floor, praying a fast prayer before answering. When she opened her eyes again, she found herself staring at the file's scattered papers.

To be exact, her father's phone ledger. She couldn't believe what she was seeing, but it wasn't the time to read it thoroughly. A final bang vibrated through the house, like the back door slamming shut, and then more silence.

She gripped the phone. "Zane could be hurt. I have to check on him."

The man snapped back. "No! Stay where you are, Ms. Perry. I mean it."

"Kristin?"

Lifting her head, she peered over the top of the desk. Zane stood in the doorway, his expression grim. She leaped up and rushed over to him. He intercepted her before she could reach the office door, catching her in his arms in a hard hug.

"Are you all right?" she asked. "I thought you'd been killed!" She cupped his face, pulling him down to her height as she checked his expression thoroughly. "Don't scare me like that again! I've lost too much in my life. I don't want you dead, too."

Kristin clamped her mouth shut and stared at Zane in shock. Of course, she didn't want him to be killed here, but the emotion in her voice rang deep and clear as the bell at the church. Did he hear how much he meant to her?

In the distance, by the phone, the security company's operator was calling out to her.

He held her gaze. "We have a problem."

"What?"

"The guy got away. He took the kitchen knife you'd laid on the counter by the back door."

"Let him have it."

"He also dropped his wallet. So, he'll either be back to get it, or disappear forever."

"Let's hope the latter."

Zane looked grim as he shook his head slowly. "I doubt it. He's from Chicago. I'm guessing he works for Martino. It's likely he'll be back to finish what he started."

FOURTEEN

Zane wished he hadn't said anything. But he couldn't exactly hide the truth from her. He'd seen the man through the broken back door window, and raced down to the basement to exit up through the narrow utility door, to come up on the man from behind.

And even though he'd been quiet enough to sneak up the steps to the back door, the person had already leaned in and grabbed the knife, most likely for extra insurance.

Zane had faced a man with two lethal weapons. He'd managed to kick the gun from the guy's hand, but not the knife.

A quick tussle and the man had managed to twist away at the last second. He'd bolted down the steps and into the woods behind the house, leaving Zane to choose to either chase him or stay with Kristin. On his way back into the house, he'd checked out the wallet the man had lost in the fight.

Zane released her. "You better talk to that guy on the phone."

"Oh!" She hurried back into the office. Zane could hear her tell how she and Zane were safe, but they needed the police. After a few more words, she hung up.

When she returned, she stared down at the man's wallet, now open in Zane's hand. "Who is he? Not one of the guys who drove into the lake, I hope."

Zane read the driver's license. "The name was Lucien Esposito. He's got an Illinois driver's license."

"Chicago, right?"

He looked at the address. "You got it."

She paled. "Whoever Lucien is he wasn't after Tammy. He'd have gone home by now because he'd already killed her." Her chin wrinkled and she bit her lip. "Tammy was killed by mistake. The poor thing. After all she'd gone through."

"They were planning to grease your palm, too, so to speak." Zane picked up a small tube of paint he'd found by the back door. "It's graphite paint, made in Chicago."

"I need to call Jackson. I know that he'll tell me off for what we've done, but he'd be a whole lot angrier if I don't say anything."

Zane tossed the paint onto the kitchen table. "Do you think that's a good idea, Kristin? That paint is from Chicago, so is our burglar, and so is Jackson McGraw. There were no attempts on your life before you visited him, and there is a leak to the Mafia from someone in the FBI or Marshal's Office. He says not to trust the police, but maybe he's the one we can't trust? Maybe he's the leak."

She shook her head. "I don't think so. While I was on the phone, I saw the rest of the stuff in that file. My father had kept this ledger of phone calls he'd made and the one number jumped out at me. It was Jackson's number! My father had called him dozens of times over the years! I don't think he would hurt me."

"You can't say that guy cares for you based on a few phone calls."

"I think he does care for me, Zane."

"Yes, I do."

Both looked up, turning toward the door leading down to the basement. Zane grimaced. He'd left the utility door open to the backyard. Now a tall man, older than Zane, with straight, slightly graying brown hair and a stern expression, stood in that doorway. "You're wrong, Mr. Black. I care very much for Kristin."

"Who are you?" Zane demanded, shifting closer to Kristin and reaching out his hand to slip her covertly behind him.

"Special Agent Jackson McGraw."

Zane looked at Kristin, then back to the agent, before allowing his gaze to slide back to Kristin. She nodded to confirm what the agent said.

Zane stepped forward. "Your ID, if you don't mind."

"Certainly." Jackson withdrew a small leather folder in which he housed his ID. "By the way, your burglar also dropped this," Jackson added. The agent held up a gun, checked it, removed the magazine and slipped both into his jacket breast pocket. "Kristin is expecting me."

Keeping half his gaze on the older man, Zane memorized the number on his ID card. Just in case.

"And I can certainly understand your suspicions, Mr. Black, or may I call you Zane? I wouldn't trust me, either, especially with the circumstantial evidence you're presenting. Very good, by the way, but then again, you were top of your class and urged to go into law, weren't you?"

Zane handed back the ID. "And you know that from whom?"

"From your instructors." He tucked his ID back into his jacket. "I wouldn't come up here unless I did my homework first."

Frowning, he stepped even closer to Kristin. "So do you know our burglar?"

"I got a glimpse of him before he ran off. I have a couple of agents chasing him. He's Lucien Esposito, as you said, a small bit player in Vincent Martino's 'family.' One of the 'soldiers.' One of the men you dragged from the lake is his capo. Some sources say Lucien has been trying for years to get into the higher ranks of the 'family,' but with no success. With this stunt, I'd say that he's still trying, hoping to get in good with the boss. Vincent Martino, I mean, not the capo. Word has it he's stepped on a few toes, even, to get ahead."

Zane didn't like this. Not only was honoring Salvatore Martino a priority, but some internal politics were involved, too. Even Kristin had only just begun to realize this fully, judging from her soft gasp.

"I'll take care of this matter," Jackson offered. He dialed a number and spoke quietly for a few minutes after turning away slightly and running his fingers through his short hair.

Then he dialed another number, spoke softly and hung up. He said, "An ambulance has been dispatched through the alarm company, but I canceled it. The police, however, are on their way. And my men lost Lucien."

"The police will be here any minute," Kristin murmured.

"It would be wise, then, for you two to leave right now," Jackson said. "I'll handle them."

"We're staying. This is my home," Kristin stated with a firm stare. "But if you like, we'll stay in the office. You'll be able to handle the police and I need to look at something in there now."

Jackson looked grim but to Zane's surprise, he acquiesced. "You'd better get in there, then, and be quiet."

"Before we go, what about the men at Lindbergh Lake?" Kristin asked. "Did they tell you anything that could help here?"

"So far, they're not talking, but," he said as he lifted the tube of paint from the kitchen table, "*this* is interesting. The last time I saw this type of paint was when we raided Salvatore's house twenty-two years ago. He'd been painting landscapes from the old country, he'd said. Salvatore had some genteel hobbies. He even hybridized roses. Surprisingly, he's good at both of them. Or he was before he fell ill."

"It's the same kind of paint on my vest. I'm sure of it," Kristin said. "And it was also on Tammy's hand."

Jackson nodded. "I know. The 'soldiers' have been using this paint to send a message to both the police and to the 'family' that each hit is a revenge hit. Tammy wasn't the first woman to be found with it on her hand unfortunately. But other victims have similar marks."

"Other victims?" Kristin echoed quietly.

"Yes, all with some kind of black grease on their hands."

Zane nodded. "Because the paint is rare and graphite grease is easier to get."

"Exactly." Jackson frowned. "Where did you get your vest tested?"

"We turned it over to the police, but it was cleaned before it was tested. Someone tampered with it right at the police station," she said. "We told them they needed to look at their own security cameras."

"But Kristin had leaned back in my car seat, and I had that sample tested," Zane added. "It was graphite paint consistent with a brand made in Chicago."

Jackson cocked his head, listening to the distant wail of a police siren. "You'd better head into the office. Stay quiet. We'll talk later."

Zane couldn't have agreed more. After Kristin told Jackson her alarm code, in case he needed it, Zane grabbed her hand and led her into her father's office.

"I wonder how he'll explain all of this to the police," Kristin murmured.

Zane locked the office door before walking to the window to shut the curtains. Then he turned on the desk lamp. "I'm sure he's dealt with the local law before. You can ask him when he's done."

"What are we going to do until then?" At her own words, heat flooded into Kristin's face. Zane could read her thoughts as easily as the evening paper. She cared for him. She wanted to be with him, to share a private moment.

With that observation, he found his own heart pounding faster. But it was hardly the time, and both knew it. To save her some embarrassment, he said, "I want to check out the Martinos plus find out who works for the FBI and Marshal's Office. Something is bugging me about this leak. And you need to check out that ledger, you said."

Kristin nodded and began to tidy up the scattered papers. "Good idea. I need to reread Dad's phone ledger before I confront Jackson about it."

Picking up his cell phone, Zane returned to the computer. Within minutes of talking to one of his contacts and searching the Internet, he had the information he was searching for.

He sat back, feeling his brows close into a frown. "Salvatore Martino is terminally ill with only a short time left to live. The search for your mother became a priority for those wanting to please the old Don." He looked up at her. "A tribute to him and to get in good with the new Don, Vincent."

"They must have learned something new, to be able to

start a fresh search." Still holding her father's phone ledger, she slumped down on her father's leather couch. It faced the fireplace and the rug she'd sprawled on for years. She blinked rapidly. Beyond, the police had arrived. Zane could hear Jackson talking to them.

Zane kept his voice low. "When people enter the Witness Protection Program, sometimes there's a fake report of that person's death. Perhaps they've recently discovered that you and your mother are still alive and now that Salvatore is dying, they want to honor him by killing both of you. But some of them have mistaken you for your mother."

"Glad to hear I look like a woman twenty years older than me," she muttered. She paused as the police and Jackson walked outside. "Maybe my parents learned what the Martino family was doing and stepped up efforts to find my mother. And kept Jackson updated. But they didn't find her."

Zane felt his heart tighten. He could handle failure to find his brother. He'd been dealing with that for two years steady, each lead he searched becoming a dead end. He really only had one lead left, prompted into action by Kristin's comment on the painting, and being worked on by a friend.

But to watch Kristin's hopes slipping further away, while her own life was at risk, was totally unfair.

Look, God, You have to care for her. Do something. Everyone needs someone in their life.

A sudden urge to be that someone in Kristin's life hit him hard with a force he couldn't ignore.

Yes, he wanted to be that someone. But it was looking more and more as if she was going to have to be hidden. And who knew where his work and his search for his brother would take him? He forced himself to admit that they'd never be able to make a relationship work.

He watched Kristin's eyes droop. "You're tired. Why don't you lie down on the couch for a while?" He rose, pulled the quilt from behind her and covered her.

She took it, but shook her head. "No, I want to look at my father's phone ledger. I want to know how often he called Jackson." She yawned. "And whoever else he called."

Before long, she was deep in studying the book. He returned to the desk and picked up his phone. There were some other things he needed to do while he had the opportunity. Things like who worked in Billings for the Marshals, and who was in the FBI office in Chicago. He had some contacts out east. It wouldn't be hard to get a list.

A while later, Zane heard a soft knock on the door. After he unlocked it, Jackson entered. Kristin stood. "Did you lock the doors? What did you tell the police about me?"

"Don't worry. Everything is fine. I locked the doors and set the alarm. I have the authority to make this break-in a federal matter and since we already have a task force in place here, there wasn't much the police could do."

Kristin's eyes widened. "You have a task force for me?"

Jackson smiled. "Not quite. It's for things related to this case."

"Were they the people who turned onto Lindbergh Lake Road? Two men and a woman?"

"They work for me, yes." The agent frowned. "But you don't need to know anything except they are looking for Martino. My first reason for coming here was to make sure you're safe, and to update both of us."

"You have news?"

"No, but I need to find out what *you've* been doing to find your mother. And don't tell me you haven't been looking. Why else were you headed to Joey Hamilton's place?"

Zane's head shot up. They'd been down that road to see where her parents had been killed, not to see Joey Hamilton. Kristin's father must have told Jackson about the reclusive P.I.

He exchanged looks with Kristin. She opened her mouth to speak, but Zane stopped her with his hand. It was unlikely that this FBI agent would make so obvious a blunder, but judging from the fatigue around his eyes, and the way his cropped, slightly spiked hair was looking a bit rough, Zane wondered if the special agent *had* slipped up.

"We weren't going to see Joey Hamilton," Zane said quietly. "We were going to see where Kristin's parents had died."

Immediately, McGraw recognized his slip. A slow smile and lowered lids gave away his resignation. Again, he drove his fingers into his short hair, then dragged them down his tired face. "But you know Joey had done some searching for Eloise."

"Now we do, but I hadn't been able to see the site after the crash. I felt the time was right, now," Kristin said gently, obviously empathizing with him for his small blunder. "In fact, I had thought it was on the other side of the Mission Mountains. I don't know why. I must have been in shock when they told me."

"But, Kristin, you evidently know about Joey Hamilton." He turned to Zane and folded his arms. "And perhaps you'd better tell me what *you* know."

She shook her head, and while she folded the quilt she'd tossed aside, Zane answered, "Look, all I could glean was from some acquaintances. He's a recluse that Kristin's parents hired to find her mother, isn't he? Is there more?"

"No. I must admit, I was half hoping there was more, but your parents refused to get their hopes up. I was the one who hoped for it each time your father called." His mouth turned grim.

"They hired Joey because he's discreet?"

"I think it had more to do with their ministry to the community, and to help his son out. Joey's mentally unstable, and I think they were praying for him, hoping God would help his mental illness. Perhaps your father had used his services years ago. I doubt we'll ever find out why they chose him."

"So they were not just going there for an update, but to minister to him?"

"That last time? As far as I could tell, yes."

Kristin looked down at her feet. "But Joey had found Tammy Lockhart, and maybe they'd gone to Missoula the day they died to see her."

"They didn't go to Missoula that day. The police investigation proved that."

"Then they must have found out that Tammy wasn't my mother and were stopping by to tell Joey." She looked up at Jackson. "And my parents regularly kept in touch with you, too, didn't they?"

"Yes. It's frowned upon, but I asked for updates, on the sly. I wanted to make sure you were all right. I'd made all the adoption arrangements, but I was just worried about you. You and your birth mother were inseparable. You were a bit of a clingy baby, I think, and I didn't want you to suffer after she left."

She smiled at him. "I understand. I imagine that my parents were concerned for me in case anything happened to them. They weren't getting any younger. Maybe that was why they were trying to find my mother."

"We may after going through your adoptive father's papers again. But remember this, Kristin. I kept in touch with your parents because I care. So you should be doing what I tell you to do."

Zane watched her carefully search the older man's face. Following her gaze, he guessed her thoughts. She was looking for a bit of herself in him. Her words confirmed his guess.

"Jackson, are you my father?"

FIFTEEN

Jackson offered her a soft smile. "No. Your father was Danny Douglas. I'm sorry to say that he's dead."

"He was named on my birth certificate, but you didn't tell me much about him so I thought my mother just wrote it down to protect you. Who was he?"

"A small-time hood that had sweet-talked his way into your mother's life before she fully realized all that he was involved in. But he died saving her. The only decent act he ever did." Jackson blinked. "I'm sorry."

Zane cleared his throat. Kristin wanted information about her mother, but there was more a pressing need than her curiosity. "The Martino family wants Kristin dead. We need a plan. We need a list of who would be after her, and a profile of each one. And we deserve to know how they've learned about Kristin."

"The Martino 'family' is big, and there are a lot of men who'd like the glory of getting the woman who put Salvatore in prison. It's Vincent who is more than a little disgruntled…"

Zane listened to Jackson trail off as his thoughts led him elsewhere. "The only reason those women like Tammy Lockhart have died is because no one knows what Eloise looks like now, or where she is. They must think she's still in the Witness Protection Program, but they've found out that Kristin is here. Regardless of whether or not they think she's her mother or herself, I want to know how that happened."

Kristin spoke. "I did everything you told me to do at the trial. I'm absolutely positive I wasn't followed when I left Chicago. You told me that the names of the visitors at the trial were never disclosed and the list destroyed."

She thought for a moment. "You also told me when you called me Monday morning that you destroyed the paper that had my contact information. I've only ever seen you and your brother, Micah, on this matter. Once, back in January when I went to Micah's work, and at the trial. To everyone else, I'm just a college student."

Jackson listened in deadpan silence. But his frown slowly deepened. She thought she could see his lips mouth a word or two, but couldn't catch what he'd so quietly said.

Zane spoke instead. "We need a plan to keep Kristin safe because regardless of the fact that you have two men in custody, Vincent Martino is on the lam and so is at least one guy looking to kill Kristin. Vincent will want to do the same."

He stared squarely at Jackson. "If he's not here in Montana yet, he'll be coming, or else you wouldn't have your task force here. And we don't know how much those guys I pulled out of the lake told him before they followed us that day."

She shook her head. "I'm not going into the Witness Protection Program, if that's what you're thinking. My mother was in it, and Tammy was in it. It's not very appealing to me right now."

"I don't blame you, but we're talking about the Martino

family. Zane is right. Martino will want to kill your mother himself, and if he knows you're Eloise's daughter, he'll deem it necessary to kill you to lure her out."

"Then we need to find my mother *now*. I know you don't want me to look for her, but we have to do something. While I was reading Dad's ledger, I was thinking that those thugs found me through that article written about my father in one of the Billings newspapers. So how did they know which newspaper to look in?"

Jackson looked thoughtful. "The Martino family knows that Eloise is in Montana. Maybe they were checking all the papers online."

"It sounds too coincidental."

"Originally, your mother was reported dead in an explosion in Montana. We didn't produce a body, so we suspect that Martino has guessed that she didn't die, but was hidden within the program. Are you sure you haven't told anyone about your search for your mother?"

Kristin blew out a sigh. "I didn't tell anyone it was my mother I was looking for. I've asked at the city hall in Missoula. I had to start somewhere so I asked at the university there."

"The whole campus?"

She looked down. "Yes. It was a long shot, I know. But even if my mother had gone there, she could be anywhere now."

"She didn't attend as Eloise Hill." Jackson looked grim, and yet, patient. "It's more likely someone saw that newspaper article."

"I'm sorry." Kristin bit her lip, and Zane knew she was near tears. Still, he watched as Jackson rubbed her arm lightly.

"It's not your fault. Knowing where you searched might help us."

Zane spoke up. "Someone is mistaking her for her mother. Those guys at Lindbergh Lake thought she was Eloise."

"And the family has actually targeted women who were younger than Eloise," Jackson added.

Kristin leaned forward. "When you found me, you took me back to Chicago. Why then give me to a family in Billings? Why not in Chicago?"

"I didn't want you anywhere near the Martino family who lived almost exclusively there. I knew your adoptive father because he'd defended an FBI agent in an accidental shooting case that went to trial. He was a good friend of my first supervisor, and a Christian, along with his wife, just what your mother would have wanted. You were meant to look like a change-of-life baby, then. So we arranged for a new birth certificate to be issued in Billings."

Zane spoke. "Look, you wouldn't assign a task force just to look for Eloise, would you?"

Jackson shot him a hooded look. *Enough,* Zane thought. If they were to protect Kristin, then they *all* needed the truth. And with that thoughtful look, and Zane's ability to read people, even this well-trained federal agent, he knew that there was more going on.

"A task force would be set up to find Martino," Zane said, "but your task force is doing more, isn't it?"

"Why do you say that?"

"Just a hunch. Task forces aren't created at random in today's tight budget times. But a task force *would* be set up to find a security leak. I was checking online how many women have died in Montana lately. This year alone there's been an increase and they're all fitting the same general description. Those women were in the Witness Protection Program, right? So someone is feeding their locations to the Mob hoping one of them is Eloise. And your task force has been set up to find who that leak is."

Jackson looked down, tilted his head slightly and glanced at Kristin. "Is it true, Jackson?" she whispered. "Is there a leak? What does that person know about me and my mother?"

"You, just a first name and age. And they only have old info on your mother. But she left the Witness Protection Program two decades ago and hasn't been seen since. Someone thinks that she's still in it, though, and we've narrowed the leak to the Billings office."

Zane gaped at him. "The Marshal's Office? There's a leak there?" It was a powerful statement for an FBI agent to admit to. And yet, Jackson's statement bugged him. Could anyone be trusted?

"The Marshal's Office wanted an independent task force, so that's where the FBI comes in. And we've also learned that whoever it is has also managed to get other government agencies to cooperate with him, making him all the more dangerous."

Jackson stopped and caught Zane's pensive stare. "What is it? Something on your mind?"

"Just something bugging me. I don't know what it is at the moment. The Marshal's Office? I can't believe there would be a leak there. That's like slicing an artery. If you don't stop it immediately—"

"I know what it means," Jackson grated out. "If you think of what's bugging you, let me know. In the meantime, let me worry about the leak. He could belong to the family. He could even be someone who knows a person with access to information on the Witness Protection Program. But we definitely know the leaked information came from Billings."

Kristin whispered, "Someone looked in the newspaper one day and saw a girl who looked like Eloise. Clay thought I looked like my mother. Do I?"

Jackson's expression softened. "Very much so. It's remarkable." Then, clearing his throat, he dug through his jacket pocket and produced a photograph. "This is a copy of the last known photo taken of your mother. I didn't show it to you before because I didn't have it handy. But remember, it's even more dangerous for you now that Salvatore is dying, and Vincent a fugitive. This photo was taken just hours before she left."

She took the photo and shared it with Zane. Though the photo wasn't the best quality, Zane could see a haunted quality about the young woman. The scar Kristin had mentioned was clearly visible.

She handed it back to Jackson. "What do we do now?"

Zane walked around to the computer and scooped up some papers he'd printed out while Kristin read. He had a ton of reading to do, if Jackson decided not to be forthcoming with information. But he also had a plan in mind.

And he knew Kristin wasn't going to like it.

"We take you to a hotel," he told her.

She shook her head. "I can't stay at a hotel anymore. I need to do things, even if it's just studying for my courses. I want to stay here. I have an updated alarm system, remember?"

"I don't think that's wise, Kristin," Jackson added.

"It is. And I deserve to stay home." She switched her firm look from Zane to Jackson and back again. "It's safe, and you're both only a phone call away. A hotel isn't necessarily safer than here. Look, I have no family, so I should be allowed to stay in the one place that reminds me of what I did have. My home. It's all I have left."

Zane wanted to remind her of what she'd gained in this past week. He wanted to remind her that she had him, and that through her presence and her own love for God he'd found his faith again. But with Jackson scowling at her, albeit in a gentle, fatherly way, he wasn't going to announce how he felt.

So he turned to Jackson. "You can bunk at my house, if you haven't got a hotel room for the night. We'll take turns watching her house. I'll do the first shift, if you like. Do you have a good picture of Martino?"

Jackson nodded. "I'll see to it you have all you need."

Zane smiled, feeling relieved. He wanted Kristin to himself, just to talk, to hold her and tell her he'd make sure she was safe.

"And," Jackson continued, oblivious to his thoughts, "Kristin, I'll find your mother if it's the last thing I do. I swear it."

She studied him, even after the older man turned away. Then she looked at Zane with a knowing lift of her eyebrows.

Yeah, he thought. With Jackson, this was personal.

Did that also make it dangerous?

Kristin watched Zane recheck the burglar alarm after Jackson had left. It also boasted a computer link, and Zane set it up using the computer in her father's office.

"This computer is the remote site. You'll see it on the desktop, and it's easy to navigate," he said, peering at the screen. "The software shows that you haven't had an incident since Jackson set the alarm and left. There's a ton of things this software can do."

Kristin was glad for the extra features. "Well, showing me will have to wait. Remember that Jake said that the default settings are fine until we're comfortable using it, and that he'll come back and show us the rest when we all have more time."

"That's a good idea. We should both be here when that happens." Zane hit the last button. Already, it was getting late. The sun had long since dipped behind the house, washing the mountains to the east in a pale pink. She used to like this time of day. Just before the bugs came out, she'd sit outside with her father. Her mother would join them after she'd tidied up the kitchen. She liked to do that by herself, her father used to say with a smile. It gave her time to pray and think on the day.

But those times were gone. And her last lead to find her mother had dissolved, too.

Lord, give us another lead. Show us the way to my mother.

All through her plaintive pray, Zane was leading her to the front door, but before opening it, he drew her into his arms. They embraced in silence for an all-too-brief moment.

"I'm sorry you haven't got a decent lead to follow," he told her gently.

She looked up at him. "I am, too. But I know we'll find her. Jackson is determined."

"He cares for her, I think."

She smiled. "I noticed that, too. And he feels responsible for what has happened. Regardless, I know that we can hope in the Lord. I'm feeling like I'm relearning how God will never leave us alone."

Zane nodded and smiled. "I'm a bit rusty in my prayers, but I'll say them tonight." His expression grew serious. "I wish things could have turned out different, Kristin. But you can always rely on me. I want to be a part of your life. I want to see you regularly."

That was the sweetest thing she'd ever heard. "We may never find our relatives. Maybe that's why God gave us each other. He's closed a door and opened a window."

"I hope not, but it's not something I would ever turn down, regardless." With his last word, he leaned down and kissed her. The warmth of his lips lingered long after he lifted his head. "Good night. Get some rest."

"What will you be doing?"

"I'll be outside in my car reading much of what I couldn't read in your office. I printed a bunch of things out."

"Like what?"

"Different lists and organizations. Where your mother might find work as a baker, and what's available on the Martino family. Understanding how the family works may help us locate Vincent. Jackson will take over around midnight. Lock the door after I leave."

She did, hating that it felt as if she was locking him out of her life. They were growing closer each day, as if a bond was knitting itself around them. Leaning against the door, she soaked herself in the feeling of being cherished. Zane hadn't said anything more than wanting to see her regularly, but it had left her feeling wanted, cared for.

After rechecking the alarm, she wandered into the kitchen for a glass of water to take upstairs. She wasn't hungry at all. She had no secret need to snack. A smile spread across her face.

Early the next morning, the phone beside her rang. She reached across her bed for it. "Hello."

"Good morning," Zane announced cheerfully.

She propped herself up on one elbow. This was nice. Really nice. They had each other to call, even early in the morning. A smile crept up to her face. "You're in a good mood."

"I am! Guess what? Remember that I had one final lead on my brother, and the man I had looking into it just called me. He's found Bobby Kendall. He's in town and wants to meet me."

SIXTEEN

Kristin sat straight up. Was she hearing him right? "Bobby Kendall wants to meet you?"

"Yes! The guy I'd hired said I should meet him right away, that I won't be disappointed."

"Right away?" she echoed. "Where are you going to meet him?"

"Jackson is still outside your place. The two of us need to talk, so I suggested out front of your house."

Here? Now? She scrambled out of bed. She wanted to be there, to see Zane finally connect with his brother. It gave her hope that, yes, maybe she would find her mother.

She hung up, and fifteen minutes later, after peeking out her living-room window to see Jackson and Zane across the street, she sat in her kitchen, toying nervously with the handle on the cup of hot coffee, waiting not so patiently for Zane to finish his talk with Jackson. Honestly, how could he seem so cool?

She was tempted to walk outside, but knew both men would hustle her back inside.

A knock at the front door dissolved any temptation. She rose, finding both Zane and Jackson standing there. She let the men in. Zane leaned forward and kissed her cheek, while Jackson watched with more curiosity than she'd noticed before.

"I guess you know who's coming," she told the older man. "I want to be with Zane when it happens."

"I expected as much. I need to touch base with my task force anyway, and Zane and I were brainstorming a bit last night about Eloise."

She led them into the kitchen and offered them both coffees. She was about to offer them some leftover pastries, but couldn't find any. Instead, she sat down again. "What did you find out?"

Zane finished the conversation. "We know that Eloise liked to bake, and could have used that talent to make a living. So I put together a few suggestions, but Jackson needs to check them out first to help to narrow it down a bit."

"Good," Jackson was saying behind her. "I'll be on my way. I'll call around lunchtime."

She plastered on a smile as she turned. "We'll check in with you, then. Be careful. If Martino is here, he'll recognize you as much as you'll recognize him."

Nodding, Jackson headed out the door. "I'll be careful."

A few minutes later, she and Zane were alone.

"You're quiet," Zane commented.

"I feel a bit overwhelmed by this. Do you really think Bobby Kendall is your brother?"

"I'm reserving judgment. It's a long shot at best," Zane answered slowly.

She shifted impatiently, and then in an effort to ease the wait, she asked, "What are the lists on my mother that you put together?"

"We compiled a list of everything we could think of, like charity bake sales, local fairs and even potluck fundraisers. Jackson will narrow it down today. Be patient."

"Easier said than done. I'm supposed to wait patiently for the Lord's timing. I guess I'm not a very good Christian." She fidgeted, trying to mask the movement by walking to the front door to peek out.

"But we just have to accept that God loves us in spite of our faults, and just wants us to trust Him to guide us?"

"You say that so well. You'd make a good missionary some day."

"I've got a good teacher."

She looked back at him. "Me? Honestly, I didn't even know how to answer your comments on God that first day we met. I'm hardly a teacher to anyone."

"You taught by your honesty and your actions, impatience included. They both line up, unlike my parents. I didn't realize that there were people like you who are trying to follow God's Will, not making it up as it suited them."

Had she really ministered to him? "*'Whoever humbles himself will be exalted,'*" she quoted. "I have no idea where in the Bible that is, but it's there somewhere."

Zane smiled at her a warm, loving smile that brought a returning one to her lips. She sucked in a breath at his beautiful smile, the happiness he was about to experience, and found herself absorbing it herself.

Right then, the doorbell rang.

Kristin jumped. As Zane walked past her, he squeezed her arm. She could feel the anticipation build in Zane as he opened the door.

A man stood, as tall and lean as Zane was, with lighter, streakier hair and a tan that seemed out of place in the cool springtime.

He stared at Zane. Then smiled broadly.

Kristin tried to breathe, but couldn't. The same smile,

the same nose, the same fluid actions as the men shook hands.

"Bobby Kendall?"

"Zane Black?"

They laughed. It was like a single sound.

Cold sluiced through Kristin in full realization of what Zane had really wanted. He'd wanted a family, even hinting that she could be his family because he never expected to find his own.

Now he had.

And seeing the look on Zane's face right now, she knew that he didn't need a woman, a lover or a wife. He wanted a family.

He'd just found that family. And, Kristin thought with a sinking heart, it didn't include her.

SEVENTEEN

Kristin could hardly move as the men talked easily together checking facts, dates, confirming that they were brothers. Her breath was stuck in her throat and she kept telling herself to force it in and out. She'd managed to deal with not being able to find her birth mother and she'd learned to deal with her parents' deaths.

She could handle this, couldn't she?

Behind her, a short noise stole her attention. But as she was about to slip away into the kitchen to avoid looking like that awkward third wheel, Zane spoke.

"Kristin, come and meet Bobby. He's been to Mexico for the winter. He's got a studio there and some of his work is hanging in galleries all over the country."

Returning, she reached out to shake the man's warm hand. He had an infectious smile, and despite the cringing feeling inside, she managed a smile back. "It's through your painting at Westbrook University that we began this search for you."

"That awful thing? I can't believe they kept it. I hate that one."

"You should send them another one," she murmured back.

He agreed, but before he could say anything more, her

phone rang. It was Jackson. She didn't want to talk to him. What if Jackson told her all their hard work hadn't panned out?

Suddenly, a part of her didn't want to look for Eloise. She didn't want to get her hopes up and worry for her mother's life should she find her. She wanted to throw up her hands and quit everything.

She let the phone ring on.

"I'll call them back," she told Zane when he looked at her.

He turned his attention back to his brother. Bobby was mentioning Mexico, how Zane could come down there with him for a few months.

And Zane's face lit up at the suggestion, enough to make Kristin turn away. He was so happy.

Suck it up, she told herself. *He's happy and you should be, too.*

On the heels of that berating, she remembered that she was losing yet another person in her life. Another person that she loved.

That hurt.

Bobby was already saying his goodbyes to Kristin. Zane needed to get home to check his e-mails, too. They'd meet later that evening.

"It was nice to meet you," he told Kristin, who was forcing out a smile. "Zane told me how you helped him track me down. I'm grateful for your help."

She shook his hand and followed him to her door. After he left, she turned to Zane. "I should call Jackson. He was the one who phoned. Looking to update me, I'm sure."

"Let's hope. I'll check in with him, too. We need to continue our surveillance tonight."

"I have a very secure home, Zane. And I know that

Jackson will stop by later to check on me. You don't need to bother."

"It's not a bother."

He took a step closer to her, but she turned and walked to the entrance to her father's office. "I'll be fine. Go spend some time with your brother."

Her words doused him like cold water. Was this it?

She drew in her breath as she spun back to face him. "Zane, you don't have to look for Eloise anymore. Jackson is here with his task force. I have all the help I need. We both saw his determination. He'll find her, I just know it."

"You hired me."

"I know, and now I'm unhiring you." She shook her head at the foolish term. "Or whatever the word is. Zane, your brother wants you to go to Mexico with him. You didn't want to take my case on in the first place, so why not go with him? You'd be a fool not to."

"It's hot in Mexico this time of year."

"Bobby's survived and I'm sure you will, too."

He felt his jaw tightening. "And what about protecting you against Martino? Where is this task force? They could be miles away."

"But Jackson isn't. And you can't tell me you can protect me any better than he can. He's an FBI agent. You're not."

He wanted to snap back that he could do as good a job as any FBI agent. He wanted to ream off the lists of qualifications he possessed. The only difference between him and Jackson was age and experience. In some ways, Zane was better qualified. He was younger, and not hindered by any rules and regulations that an FBI agent might be.

But he held back his irritation. More was going on here

than what appeared. "I agreed to find your mother, and I don't shirk my duty."

"Your brother is waiting, Zane. Don't keep him."

"Never mind my brother. He can wait. He doesn't strike me as the impatient sort. Why are you giving up on finding your mother, all of a sudden?"

She threw up her hands. "I can't ever find her! It's too dangerous. For her and for me! Look around you, Zane. Look at all we've done and all that's happened. A woman has been murdered! I don't dare find my mother and risk both our lives! If she thought it was safe to find me, she would have years ago. Obviously, she didn't think it was safe to do that. And I won't risk seeing her for only a few minutes, and then lose her again forever! I won't!"

Her chin wrinkled as she fought to control her emotions. She turned and rushed away.

He found her in the kitchen, struggling to yank tissues from a box, and muttering when they ripped on her. "Stupid box."

"Kristin!"

She turned around. "You should go. I don't know what the neighbors are thinking of me. First you, then you and Jake, then you and Jackson, then you and Bobby. I'm surprised that the pastor hasn't come to check on me."

"That didn't bother you before." He grabbed her shoulders and squared her off to him. "What's really going on here?"

"Finding my mother is just not meant to be. I can feel it. The way God is telling me to back off. I'm sorry, Zane. I didn't mean to mislead you with hiring you, but I've come to see how wrong this search is. Jackson will find her eventually. I was wrong to involve you in all this and waste your time. Send me your bill when you get back to your office. I mean it, Zane. Get out of here."

The blow was crushing, stealing his breath and tightening around him like an iron band.

"No, Kristin," he said, quietly focusing on her completely, all the while keeping himself from tightening his grip on her shoulders. "I took your case because I wanted to. You haven't misled me."

"Yes, I have," she answered, her voice plaintive and barely above a whisper. "Finding my mother is just not meant to be. I knew it, but was being defiant about getting what I wanted."

"Like you knew that you weren't missionary material? Like you knew you could never minister to me and my jaded view on God? Look at what you've taught me. Not in the traditional sense, but with your own faith, your own actions."

She shook her head. "I've done nothing, and you know it. Now you have your family, just as I prayed you would."

"You're not the only one who prayed. I prayed all the way over here today that Bobby would be my brother. I wasn't making deals with God in some backhanded, sarcastic way that I had before. And all the way here, I knew He was in control. I can't explain it any better than that. It's just something I know. I've learned to trust God, and accept His Son only because of your faith."

He released her, trying to quell his sudden frustration. What was really going on here? He prided himself in reading body language, but suddenly, he couldn't read hers. He couldn't fathom what was going on in her head. Her face was more a mask to him than anyone's had ever been before. Her reasons were clouded, too.

All he could think of was how she didn't want him in her life anymore. And he didn't understand why.

But he would finish what he'd promised he'd do. Only then would he consider Bobby's offer of traveling to Mexico with him.

If he wanted to.

"Forget it," he muttered. He still had his own sense of commitment.

She frowned at his short, tight words, but said nothing. After a long, anxious minute, he spoke. "I will find your mother, because that's what you hired me to do." Then, before he said anything he might regret, he stalked out of the house and shut the door a bit too heavily.

EIGHTEEN

Kristin slumped against the wall, shut her eyes and listened to Zane's departure. A car door slammed, then a car started and backed out of her driveway.

She'd lost him. She'd thought she'd made that special connection with him, and for a while, maybe she had. It had been wonderful, comforting, exciting. She'd had someone to love and a strong chance of finding her mother, but all of that was just a fanciful dream. The reality of life had been flung to the ground in front of her.

She loved him, but it was all just a one-sided fantasy.

Dejectedly, she opened the freezer above her refrigerator. She shouldn't be reaching for food again. Good thing there wasn't much in there. But when had she eaten the pastries she'd baked and frozen a couple of weeks ago, the ones she'd wanted to offer to Zane and Jackson?

She slammed the freezer door just as the phone rang. Wiping her tears, she hurried into the living room to answer it. "Hello?"

Jackson didn't like the tone of Kristin's voice. She sounded defeated, a dangerous attitude. "If you have a few minutes, I'd like to talk. You didn't answer your phone earlier."

"I'm sorry. Zane and his brother were here. It was a good reunion, albeit short. They'll get together later." Her words sounded guardedly hopeful. He hated that he didn't have the ultimate good news for her, like Zane had received, but still, what he had was better than nothing.

Shifting his cell phone to the other ear, he sat back in his car and watched her house. He'd seen the man who could only be Zane's brother arrive, followed shortly by the brother and then Zane leaving. "I've done some searching and have found something."

"I've told Zane he doesn't need to search anymore. He should spend time with his brother." Her tone was flat, but still, she asked, "What have you discovered?"

"We hadn't considered Eloise's talents before because we didn't really know of any, but baking for money is quite possible. Another thing is that Eloise would know that she shouldn't take a job related to her previous life."

"She was just a kid in that foster home. The Mafia wouldn't know that she liked to bake, would they?"

"Probably not, but considering we have a security leak…"

"They may know all we know? How? I haven't told anyone about her baking abilities."

Nor had he, which made their investigation all the more difficult. Still, he didn't want to give her reason to give up any more than she already had. He understood how she felt. She was lonely.

And so was he. He was tired of work, and tired of being alone, and tired of not knowing where Eloise was. Finally, he spoke. "But we hadn't considered that she might bake for fairs, or contests, or even church, if she still attends one."

"I hope so. My faith has been the only continuing comfort to me through all of this."

Jackson knew Kristin was a believer. After all, he'd had

contact with her parents over the years. Illegal contact, if some bureaucrat nitpicked, but he didn't care. Eloise had left her baby in his care, and he didn't shirk his duty. She'd had a strong faith, and she wanted her child to have faith, too.

He wouldn't ever treat anything Eloise asked him with triviality. And having her daughter become a Christian would make her very happy.

Grimacing, he spoke again. "Kristin, I've been checking out the local area."

"What for?"

"Fairs, exhibitions, craft shows and all the things that Zane suggested. I've narrowed the search down considerably. I was going on the premise that your mother would enter a few competitions, and maybe earn a bit of extra money, in case she was afraid to actually work as a baker."

"What did you find?"

"We found one fair in particular has a big purse to win in its baking section. It's a huge event, and it's starting tomorrow."

She gasped. "Tomorrow! I don't know of any fair this early in the year. Most around here are in the late summer or fall."

"It's more a craft exhibition and summer kickoff than anything else. It runs for five days, south of here. But it has big money prizes for baking, preserves and even has a juried art show and new inventions section. And past winners include a rather mysterious woman whom we can't locate."

A silence lingered through the phone. Was she going to tell him she didn't want to keep searching, as he was sensing she might?

"Kristin?"

"I was prepared to tell you to go home, Jackson. I told Zane that I wanted to give up because I'm scared I'll be disappointed and lose her like I've lost Mom and Dad and Z—"

What had happened between those two? A fight? He couldn't see Zane giving up on her, no more than he could see Kristin giving up.

She drew in a deep breath. "But I can't. Not when we've come so far. When do we leave?"

Her question was anticipated. He just hadn't expected it to come in such a way that he felt as if he was about to kick a puppy. "You're going to stay home. This is too dangerous for you. I'm arranging for a guard—"

"My mother will be there!"

"Your mother *may* be there. That's a lot different. I won't risk you. If Martino and his 'family' know as much as we know, they'll be there to take advantage of the situation. By grabbing you, they may hope to force your mother to reveal herself. You're staying at home. I'll arrange for one of my task force to stay with you. Thea is her name. You'll like her."

"I'm sure I would if I was to stay home, but I think I'll be safer with you and the whole task force around me. No doubt you'll be taking the rest of this task force with you, anyway, right?"

She still amazed him. For being a sheltered, naïve woman, she was smart. Living with a lawyer and a teacher had taught her well. She had a logical mind. "It's still not as safe as your house," he said.

"I disagree, and I think you do, as well. You don't trust the local law enforcement, so you'd only be satisfied if one of your task force stayed with me, but then you'd be losing a valuable member, and you don't want that."

Her adoptive father's daughter. No genetic ties, but

she'd learned well how to argue her case. He watched a family in a minivan pull into a house across the street. Several young teens spilled out and were halfway to the front door before their parents called them back to help with the groceries. A nice, normal family, the envy of anyone like him. "I'm not willing to risk you."

"It's because I'm Eloise's daughter and you feel responsible for me. But, Jackson, put yourself in my shoes. I *need* to find my mother and as much as I was ready to give up, I can't now that you've told me this about the fair. We have to risk this, or more women will die." Her voice softened. "I don't want to be alone anymore. Don't you understand?"

Oh, he understood, all right. All those days and nights, sometimes when he was staking out a place, or checking out lonely areas, or watching other lonely people, he'd think of Eloise and wonder what she was doing.

Was she thinking of him as he was thinking of her?

Kristin didn't want to be alone. What about Zane? He'd talked to the man just before calling Kristin, and the guy had sounded terse and angry when he'd flatly told him that Kristin didn't want him to continue his search.

Part of Jackson had been relieved, but Zane had become invaluable to Kristin, and subsequently so to Jackson. He wasn't going to let the private investigator off the hook so easily, no matter what was going on between him and Kristin. He'd told Zane to be prepared to come tomorrow. No arguments.

"I'm not going to commit to taking you anywhere right now, Kristin. I'll need to make some arrangements first. We need to get a layout of the fair, see what they have for security, and I have to meet with my task force before I make a final decision."

"Where is this fair?"

"South of Missoula, Mountain—" He stopped and sighed, knowing that a part of him was going to berate the rest of him for his next decision. She was resourceful. She'd find it anyway, and he had no legal right to detain her.

"All right. I'll tell you all about it on the way. Its biggest prize goes to the pie baking contest winner."

"Clay said she could bake a mean huckleberry pie." Her tone changed. "Be honest with me here. What are the chances that my mother will be at this fair?"

He honestly didn't know, nor could he pull out a statistic and give her false hope. And if he said the chances were slim, she might not take his security seriously. "I don't think about percentages, Kristin. It's a strong lead, and I know that Eloise would do what she could to survive, and in order to survive, she'd need money. This would be an opportunity to get some big money. But she may not be there, for any number of reasons."

Kristin nodded. "I understand. And, yes, I don't want to get my own hopes up too high, either." Her words were calm, sweet, even. But the underlying emotions burned strong. "I'm going with you. So please don't think you can sneak away without me. I'll be at that fair, either with you and your task force or by myself."

He lifted his brows in amusement at her changed tone. "That's a little stubborn, isn't it?"

"Whatever you may think, I'm not stubborn. Stubbornness is not a good trait, no matter how you describe it. But I do know what I need to do. I need my mother and what if the Lord is guiding me to her even if I thought differently earlier."

"Then why didn't the Lord just deliver her to you years ago?"

She let out a soft, sad sound. "Because I'm meant to meet

some incredible people before that happens. People like you."

He grimaced. He wasn't incredible. He was tired of his work, and frustrated that Eloise had so successfully hidden herself. God wasn't guiding people when there were men like the Martinos around.

"Jackson, call me to let me know when you're leaving, okay?"

She hung up.

Jackson shut his phone. He wondered if Eloise was as difficult as her daughter was. He was expecting her to be, now.

Abruptly, the phone rang. He flipped it open and answered, "McGraw here."

"Big Mac, it's me." It was Roark Canfield, one of his task force members. The tough, rugged man always called Jackson "Big Mac," knowing full well how much it irritated him. "We found where Lucien Esposito has been staying. He's disappeared but you need to see what he's left behind."

"I'll be right there."

Kristin grimaced as she set down the phone and walked to the front hall. She wasn't stubborn, and she hated stubbornness. So why did Jackson's words rattle her so much?

Because Zane had called her stubborn when they first met in that café, a voice told her.

She set her house alarm. Naïve, yes, but no, not stubborn.

Outside her house, a vehicle screeched its tires as it raced down the street. No doubt that family across the street had allowed one of their teenagers to have their van.

Irritated, she grabbed her purse, with the intent to drop

it onto her bed and start some much-needed housework. She grabbed her laundry hamper as she passed the bathroom.

From inside her purse, "Ein Kleine Nachtmusik" danced out as her phone rang. Pausing, one arm around her hamper, she dug out the phone and stared at the screen.

Zane.

She didn't want to talk to him. What would he say to her? That he was leaving for Mexico after all?

Her throat tightened as the music played on. She was happy for them both, but could she endure being the third wheel, left out of the family circle because she had none?

No, she couldn't.

Still, the urge to hear his voice one more time gripped her hard and fast.

Her finger poked the talk button.

"Kristin?"

Zane's voice was filled with concern. Her heart pounded, and regret ripped through her at the way she'd sent him packing. She should have been more compassionate, stronger, smarter and less naïve in realizing that Zane had only wanted a family. If she'd figured that out sooner, it wouldn't hurt as it did now.

"I'm here. What's wrong?"

She heard a sigh of relief. Hefting up the hamper, she walked around to the basement stairs.

"I've been listening to the police scanner. They've found where Lucien Esposito's been staying, but he hasn't been seen there in a day or two. They're collecting some evidence right now."

She paused halfway down the basement stairs. "Of course he'd keep a low profile. You chased him away."

"I don't have too many details yet, but I know that the

Marshal's Office has been at that motel, too. Someone from there has been feeding the Martino family information on Witness Protection women. And on you. Remember, Lucien Esposito wants to kill you."

All business, she thought. No warm, comforting words expressing that he'd rather stay with her than go to Mexico with his brother. Nothing about the relationship they'd been building.

Still, he did call. And his words began to sink in. "What does all that mean now?"

"You should leave. Let me call Jackson—"

She finished walking down the stairs. "I'm fine here until the morning. Did Jackson tell you about the fair? He just called—"

She turned the corner toward the washer and dryer.

Then jumped. Two men stood beside the washer, one with his hands wrapped around a large gun.

One of the men looked very familiar.

She gasped.

It was Lucien Esposito.

NINETEEN

Automatically, she rammed the hamper into the men. A shot from the gun went wide as the weapon was knocked to the floor. The unarmed man grabbed the hamper and tossed it aside. Kristin spun, but was caught by the arm and whirled back around and slammed against the nearby wall. Her cell phone dropped to the floor and skittered out of reach.

She could feel the meat of Esposito's fist skim past her nose on its way to the thick concrete wall of the basement. She slunk down until she hit the cold floor. Her hip fell onto the gun.

Esposito's knuckles plowed into the concrete wall. The man cried out and pulled his bleeding hand in close to his chest. The other man tossed one of Kristin's dirty towels to him, which Esposito grabbed and wrapped it around his knuckles.

Kristin knew she'd never make it past both men, but she had the advantage of being closest to the gun, and the appearance of being semiconscious.

"Where's my gun?"

"I dunno, Lucien. It's gotta be here somewhere."

"Find it, or when I find it, I'll use it on you!"

The man straightened and pulled on his friend's arm. "Hey, get off my back, all right? You're the one who called me."

"Shut up! I need my gun."

"You shouldn't have stayed here all night. You were bound to get caught."

"I said, shut up!"

"We should go. Your hand needs looking after—"

"No! I want this woman dead! I want Vincent Martino to know who he can count on. You want to make a bit more money, too, don't you?"

"Sure, but I can take care of this woman. No one knows me here."

"Forget it! I want to kill her myself!"

"You should hand her over to Vincent. He'll thank you good for that."

Kristin dared to open her eyes. Lucien Esposito loomed over her, his expression dark and furious. He was wiping the blood from his knuckles. She could still feel the throb from where they skimmed her cheek.

She didn't know the other man, but it was obvious that he had been promised some things if Lucien was promoted.

"I want my gun, moron. Now!"

The man scrambled to his task, throwing Kristin's scattered laundry about in his haste to find the weapon. Esposito stood nearby, cradling his towel-wrapped hand.

The other thug circled past her again to toss aside a large box. In it were the effects from her parents' car. She'd dried it all out, then set it all into a box, out of sight.

Everything her parents had taken that fateful day skittered across the basement floor.

Straightening up, the thug said, "I can't find it."

They both turned to her. She half lay there, pretending

to be unconscious, pretending not to hear and understand what was being said.

Esposito stepped menacingly closer. "Get up!"

Kristin opened her eyes to face that horribly evil man. She tried to mouth a prayer, but nothing vocal came. At a loss, she began to think the twenty-third psalm.

The Lord is my shepherd. I shall not want.

Esposito flung away the bloodied towel, and grabbed the front of her shirt. He fisted his bleeding hand, swung back and twisted his mouth into something thin and ugly.

Then a blur of dark colors flew down the stairs. The two men spun at the last second, not enough time to react.

It was Zane! Both men landed in a heap on the dirty clothes and her parents' effects. Zane straddled Esposito, hitting the man with some kind of downward thrust that rendered the man immediately unconscious.

Kristin skidded away from the other man, who had paused long enough to allow her such a movement. Her hip hurt from the hard gun beneath her, but she gritted her teeth against the pain as she dragged it with her.

Zane leaped to his feet, but not before the other man shoved him away. Then the thug galloped up the stairs, twisting only once to kick at Zane.

He missed. Zane easily deflected the kick, and was about to gallop up the stairs, but Esposito staggered to his feet and swung around to face Kristin.

Reacting, Zane tackled him again. Kristin knew he'd made a choice between protecting her and going after that other man.

Relief washed through her like cold water at the choice he'd made. Then she felt her head hit the floor.

"Kristin? Kristin, open your eyes."

She blinked open her eyes to find Zane peering down

at her. She was lying on the basement floor. The gun Esposito had aimed at her still dug into her hip.

She brought those around her into focus. Zane, Bobby, even Jackson. "Lucien Esposito was here! With some other guy! Did you catch them?"

Zane shook his head. "No. Bobby chased them, but lost them somewhere in the neighborhood. Jackson has his task force searching." He looked relieved and worried at the same time. "You didn't hang up your cell phone, and I could hear everything."

Jackson appeared beside Zane. She sat up, wincing at the pain. Zane stilled her. "You've been out for a few minutes. How do you feel?"

"A bit achy, but I will probably feel worse tomorrow." She touched her cheek. "Do I have a bruise?"

"Not yet."

She rolled over and lifted up the gun. "Esposito dropped this. Then I fell on it."

Jackson took it. "How did they get in?"

"Lucien has been in here all this time."

Zane cleared his throat. "He had the code. Lucien must have slipped back in through the basement door after he fled into the woods yesterday. The only time you said your code aloud was to Jackson. He's been hiding in the furnace room down here."

She sagged against the cold wall.

"I should have locked that door as soon as that guy took off," Zane growled.

Jackson moved away to flip out his cell phone. Kristin could hear him call Micah, his brother who she'd been taken to by another Marshal when she went to Billings to ask about her mother. They must be sharing information.

She turned to Zane, but turned her head away quickly.

There were words she ached to say to him, but she held them back. Instead, she focused on brushing herself off.

Zane led her to one of the spare dining-room chairs that were stored down here. "Kristin, what's going on? You practically shoved me out the door today, and now you don't want to talk to me? Let's face it, you didn't want to answer when I called your cell phone. It rang too many times."

She glanced around the basement. Jackson was busy on the phone. When he caught the two staring at him, he walked upstairs.

Once alone, Zane focused on Kristin, making her squirm nervously. "Kristin, why didn't you want to answer my call?"

"What was there to say? You had promised to find my mother, even though I told you not to, and you'd already found your brother, so what else did we need to discuss?"

He gaped at her. "What do you mean, what else? What about us? About the way you're treating me?"

"Are you going to Mexico with Bobby?"

He straightened. Then, dragged his hands down his face. With a sigh, he pulled up another chair and sat beside her. In the quiet of the room, they could hear Jackson and his colleagues talking upstairs.

"That's what this is all about, isn't it?"

Her heart pounding, she stared at her hands. She didn't want to be dumped in her basement. Hadn't she gone through enough today? Couldn't it wait until tomorrow?

Lord Jesus, help me accept what's about to happen.

Zane took her hand. "Kristin, look at me."

She lifted her head, but he swam in a wash of tears. Wordlessly, he pulled a tissue from his pocket and handed it to her.

"I'm sorry," she mumbled, not liking the silence all of a sudden. "Crying is so stupid, and yet, I keep doing it!"

"It's all right. I understand. More than you know."

She didn't answer.

"Kristin, wipe your tears, and listen to me."

"No, Zane. I don't want you to say anything. I appreciate all you've done for me, and I'm happy for you that you've found your brother, but it's time to move on. For both of us."

"And your mother? What about her?"

Kristin shrugged. "Jackson has an idea on where to check for her. I trust him to find her and apprehend Martino and his men before anything else happens. I don't want you involved. You're the one who has found your family."

"And I want you to share in it."

"I don't want to be the third wheel."

"You won't be. You're special to me. You helped me let go of my anger toward God."

She searched his face. That was it? Nothing more?

Why should there be? He knew she'd guessed she was being dumped and was only letting her down gently here.

Because so much was happening to her. But she could handle this. Lifting her chin, she tried to stay businesslike, "Jackson called me earlier to tell me about the fair that he believes my mother may visit. There's a big money prize in the baked goods contest, and he has a good feeling about this one. I have to go with him."

"I don't imagine any of us will be able to stop you. You realize that I'm going with you, too, don't you?"

Before she could answer, Jackson trotted down the basement stairs. His expression was grim.

"We've ordered a canine unit in to follow the blood trail Esposito has left. The Marshal's Office is on the way, too."

Kristin caught the short, furtive look that Zane and Jackson exchanged. "Is that wise?" she asked. "Someone there is leaking info on me." There was lingering in the back of her mind, but she couldn't pull it out.

Jackson cocked his head. "Which means it's time we turned the tables."

She couldn't believe what she'd just heard. "You're going to leak out that we're going to the fair?"

"Yes. I'll brief you tonight on it. If the Martino family learns of it, we have to be ready for them." Jackson turned to head back up the stairs. But Zane's frown deepened when Jackson shot one last knowing look at him.

"It's called 'The Heart of the Mountain' Fair, at Mountain Springs," Jackson said that evening after the police had left and the dust had settled. He'd brought with him an attractive young woman named Thea. Jackson introduced her as his computer expert who just happened to be able to run faster than him. Kristin studied the young woman, recognizing her from the rest stop near Lindbergh Lake. She'd thought that they seemed a bit out of place in this rugged backcountry.

"You work for Jackson?" she asked Thea.

"In a manner of speaking, yes." Thea smiled at all of them. "Is there something wrong?"

"No. I saw you at that rest stop near Lindbergh Lake. You came in with two men. Were you headed up to Westbrook?"

"We were in the area when Jackson called us," she answered guardedly.

Kristin peeked over the table at Zane, catching the look on his brother Bobby's face. He was staring at Thea with fascination.

But the beautiful FBI agent was all business.

"We're still waiting on the layout of the fair," she added to Jackson's comment as they all sat down around the dining-room table. Kristin had ordered in pizza and the smell of it and those cinnamon fingers that came with the order made her mouth water. She set them as far as possible from her.

"We haven't been able to confirm who's entered what competitions yet, either, but I expect we'll know by later tonight."

"They may not know everyone because some enter the contests at the last minute," Bobby warned, reaching for a piece of pizza, "and some drop out if their baking doesn't turn out well. The lists aren't accurate, except for the juried art show. They need to have the artwork up and judged the day before. The baking is done the first day of the fair."

Zane frowned at his brother. "How do you know this?"

"I've entered it a few times." He smiled at Thea. "In fact, I may be able to help you here. The baked goods competition allows for last-minute entries. They discovered that they get more entrants that way."

"How many times have you been to this fair?" Jackson asked.

"Four or five times. I entered one of my paintings last year, and won second place in the mixed media. Plus one year, I tried my hand at the bread contest, but couldn't compete with some of these longtime bakers.

"But I know the fairgrounds pretty well. If we're looking for a good baker, then I say you check out the open competition instead of the pie baking one."

"Why?" Jackson checked his paperwork. "The pie division has a higher prize."

"Not really. The open competition has a dessert division

where the winner receives a pretty good-size award, *and* it automatically becomes eligible to be judged in the best in the show category, whereas the pie division isn't considered for that. And the winner of the best in show then receives an extra thousand dollars."

Kristin looked to Jackson, who looked at Thea. She was already in the process of flipping open her laptop. Still ignoring Bobby's silly grin, she quickly searched her files. "He's right. And with the open competition, they say that you can enter the contest right up until an hour before judging."

"Which could mean," Kristin said, hating how her hopes were rising. She'd told herself not to get caught up in this. "That my mother would have a bit more anonymity. No one would know she was there until she entered the competition."

Her heart seemed lodged in her throat, and she had to swallow the last of the iced tea to relieve the anticipation. Finally, unable to control her swelling hopes, she rose and grabbed the empty pitcher to refill it.

Zane followed her into the kitchen and watched her dig out the iced tea from the refrigerator. "It's okay to feel optimistic," he said quietly as the other three discussed the new revelation. "This is all falling into place. Just have a bit of faith, okay?"

She nodded. Then, placing the full pitcher down on the counter, she said, "It's just that the way things are working out, it's all so amazing. We found your brother, and he's turning out to be a godsend to us. Who'd have thought?" Her voice cracked. "My faith is secure, but I'm afraid that God will answer with a no."

Zane pulled her into a tight embrace, just as Jackson's cell phone rang. Kristin could hear him answering it, but clung to Zane without listening to the older man's soft words. This was her moment with Zane. She rested her head against his shirt and prayed that what they were doing was God's will, and that He didn't have something else planned.

She forced optimism into her thoughts. Tomorrow she might finally meet her mother. And with Zane and Jackson, they'd both be safe. What could possibly go wrong?

Jackson walked into the kitchen. He said nothing for a moment, instead letting his frown deepen. Clearing her throat, Kristin peeled herself away from Zane.

"That was my office. Salvatore died early this afternoon."

"Oh."

"He died in hospital, asking for his son. The capos pulling a vigil at his bedside are said to be very furious."

"At what?"

"At not being able to kill Eloise earlier. And you, too."

"That's good for my mother, and for me, isn't it? I mean if they wanted to pay tribute to him by killing my mother, then it's too late for that, isn't it?"

Jackson shook his head. "The opposite, I'm afraid. Vincent Martino will be even more determined to get your mother now. This has moved from a tribute killing to a revenge killing."

"My mother didn't hurt Salvatore."

"No, but his health failed after he was incarcerated, which was Eloise's fault. Vincent will blame Eloise for that."

His expression turned even grimmer. "And revenge makes a person a whole lot more determined."

TWENTY

The fair smelled delicious. Kristin's parents had hated the cloying scent of cotton candy and fried food, but she'd always loved the whole ambience.

Today, though, her stomach stayed in a knot, tightening progressively as the minutes ticked by. She was scared. Scared for her mother, for those who may be hurt by the Martino family.

Last night, Bobby had hunkered down with Jackson and Thea, partly because the sultry woman had besotted him without even knowing it, and by the time they were done, all of them were well acquainted with the fair's layout, the Martino family's habits and Martino's many photographs.

Kristin wanted to head straight for the baked goods tent, but Zane held her back.

"We don't want to call attention to ourselves," he whispered. "No one is headed there yet."

"Okay, but it's hard." Kristin flicked the brim of her ball cap. She'd shoved her hair through the back hole and tied it up into a messy ponytail. With the dark glasses hiding the bruise Esposito had inflicted, and the bulky drab sweatshirt, she felt like a completely different person.

Jackson leaned over closer to her. "Just humor us, okay?"

She nodded and they wandered onto the fairgrounds. Ahead, the midway drew people with its bright flashing lights and bold music. Children dashed past them.

"Look," Jackson said, drawing Kristin's attention to the tent ahead. A sign out front announced that judging was in progress and the baked goods division would be opening in an hour.

Anticipation building in her, Kristin scanned the crowd, searching out each woman's face.

But not seeing anyone who looked like her.

"What are we going to do for an hour?" she muttered.

"We could see the juried art show," Bobby suggested, his eyes on Thea.

Kristin felt a pang of sympathy for the man. Thea had not given him a single hint of interest, but he kept on trying. "Why not?" she asked with a shrug. "It's right across from the baked goods tent, and one of us could stand outside and keep an eye on it."

"I will," Jackson volunteered, slipping on sunglasses. "I'd be looking like a bored husband waiting on his wife."

Thea grinned and patted his arm. "Good. Your training is going well. You'll make a good husband someday."

He shot her a dark glare. "Never mind my training. Just remember yours."

He was anxious, Kristin noticed. Not nervous, but rather so vigilant he looked as though he'd snap in half.

With raised brows, Thea led them into the tent. Rows of paintings and small sculptures filled the large tent. Someone had erected tall, white office dividers to cordon off sections, and the crowd was thickening quickly. Zane and Kristin followed Bobby as he pointed out the works of various artists he knew. Thea hovered behind them.

Kristin stopped at a painting similar to the one she'd seen at the university. "This looks like yours," she told Bobby.

They studied it before Kristin peered around the wall to see what was next, all the while hoping there were some whose subjects weren't mountains and sky and horses. Maybe something more Early American—

A man ahead turned slightly, catching her eye before disappearing around the next white corner.

Martino! She slipped quickly back behind the wall, her hand moving up to her mouth. "Zane!" she whispered. "Come here!"

Zane was immediately beside her. Thea hurried close, too.

"Martino was just over there!"

Thea was already on the small two-way radio to Jackson. She'd clipped it on her cuff. Was the whole task force here?

Zane grabbed her and dragged her back around the corner. He focused briefly on his brother. "We've got to get out of here. Now!"

Bobby sobered quickly. "I agree. We'll be safer outside."

"Let's go, then." Zane latched on to her hand and hurried her out of the tent. At the entrance, Jackson took a hold of her other hand and they began to move into the thickening crowd that strolled the main promenade.

"Wait!" she snapped out quietly. Before Jackson could hurry her off the fairgrounds, Kristin stopped dead in her tracks. Ahead, the sides of the baked goods tent were being rolled up. Immediately, Jackson began talking into his mic, telling them to watch the juried art tent for Martino.

"Forget the contest, Kristin. We need to get you out of here. I'll come back—"

"No, they're ready to give out the prizes!" She turned to him, still holding Zane's hand in her left one, and Jackson's in her right. "We've come too far to leave now."

"Kristin, you agreed to follow my rules."

"I am." The crowd had closed around them, and they were boxed in by a mass of people, all who were staring up at the baked goods tent. When he said nothing, she added, "If we move away now, we'll be going against the crowd. We'd stick out like sore thumbs and Martino is sure to spot us."

Jackson considered her words, as Kristin pressed on, "I won't do anything, I promise. But you want to find Eloise as much as I do, right? Please. She means as much to you as she does to me. Let's see if she's here, just for a moment?"

But Jackson wasn't listening. He stood staring at the baked goods tent, his expression slackened. His grip on her hand tightened. He paled, as if he was going to faint.

"What's wrong?"

"Don't move a muscle, Kristin. If Martino is here, anything we do will give Eloise away."

Her heart tripped up in speed. "How?"

"Because," he whispered, leaning close to her, "your mother is right there."

She gasped.

"Don't move, Kristin," he begged. "Please don't move a muscle."

She nodded. Relief swamped across the man's face, and still gripping her, he added, "Don't give her away."

Kristin blinked hard, fighting the tears as she ached to turn around to look. "Are you sure?"

"Absolutely positive." He touched his earpiece. "My agents have lost Martino for the moment."

Kristin bit her lip, and shut her eyes. "Zane—"

Zane released her hand and wrapped his arm around her shoulder. "Do as he says, sweetheart. Let the crowd thicken."

"Then I won't be able to see her. I'm too short!" She hiccupped out a small sob. Zane tightened his grip. By now, Jackson wasn't facing the tent ahead, the one that they'd just rolled up the side to reveal a table filled with awards and baked goods. He was facing Kristin talking softly into his mic. She stared back at him, unable to breathe, knowing that the contestants had moved in around the awards.

Jackson looked grim. "Martino was just spotted in the parking lot. He—"

Behind her, Zane whispered a soft, "Whoa."

She couldn't stand it anymore. Following his gaze with her eyes only, she was met with an incredible sight.

"She looks like me!" Though her words were barely a whisper, she knew Zane heard her.

"Yes. She's beautiful. Just like her daughter. I look forward to meeting her."

"Which won't be today," Jackson whispered harshly. "Not with Martino close. Right, Kristin?"

She nodded, barely able to move.

"I know you want to meet her, but we have to move carefully. I need to intercept Eloise when she's done. I promise, Kristin, you'll meet her soon. But in the meantime, we follow my rules. We don't need any more deaths."

"No. I can wait."

She bit her lip to stop herself from crying out.

Her mother.

Her mother was right there, accepting the award for her huckleberry pie, and it won best in the show, too. As the crowd clapped, someone handed her a blue ribbon and she smiled warmly back at the judge. She had lovely hair, the same color as hers. She was so delicate, so youthful.

She looks so much like me. Thank You, Lord. For everything.

Kristin bit her lip to hold back her tears. Finally, she dragged her gaze away. "I'll do whatever you say, Jackson. I know my mother is alive. And with Zane here—" she smiled up at him warmly, finding that though he swam in her unshed tears, he was clearly as moved as she was "—I've learned that I'm so much more than I thought I could ever be."

Zane kissed her hair, and crushed her in a loving embrace. Jackson spoke into his mic as furtively as possible. Then they filtered through the thinning crowd. When she glanced back at her mother, the woman was melting back into the crowd. Jackson was again talking on his mic, telling someone that Martino had sideswiped the parking attendant's hut as he sped away. Kristin hiccupped a small sob.

"It won't be long, sweetheart," Zane whispered as they slipped to the side of the crowds. Safe behind the front entrance, he added, "We'll meet her, and you'll have your whole future with her."

They watched one of Jackson's men then tear away from the fair in pursuit, but Jackson's expression was grim. Kristin knew the odds of catching Martino were slim.

"We? What about your going to Mexico with Bobby?"

"I thought about it. I thought about everything you said yesterday." Understanding lit up his face. Then he let out a soft laugh. "You've been hurting, afraid to hope for success in finding your mother, afraid that I would drop you as soon as I found my brother. That's not going to happen. You think that *I've* been looking for a family all this time and now that I have my brother, I don't need you anymore."

"You need a family." Even as she said that, she cringed inwardly. And held her breath.

"I have one in you, Kristin. I love you and want to marry you. I want to spend the rest of my life with you, and I'm willing to wait for you." He chuckled. "I've learned to trust God, and I see that I've learned patience, too."

"I know. Something I need to learn. Wait upon the Lord, the Bible says."

"Yes. When the time is right, we'll meet your mother. Sometime in the near future."

Kristin hugged him back. "And in the meantime, we have *our* future together."

* * * * *

Dear Reader,

When I was writing this story, I had to access memories I'd kept locked away for a long while. These memories included the deaths of my parents, and how alone I had felt. Of course, no matter how good one is at writing, no one can ever fully explain the feeling of losing a parent. A woman who was in her sixties once told me that no matter how old you are, when your mother passes away, it hurts terribly and you feel like a small child again.

In *Fatal Secrets,* my heroine deals with great loss. Her beloved adoptive parents have died and, months later, she's still struggling.

But she has her faith, and with that we can know that God is there to comfort you, and can do an amazing thing for your grief. No, He doesn't take it away. But the pain is eased, and the knowledge that God loves everyone, that He wants to welcome those who have passed away with open arms, makes the tough times ahead easier.

My heroine also discovers another important truth. That God is working actively in her life and in Zane's life, right to the very point that He wants them together. We can do so much for each other on earth. It all starts with trust in God, and love for others, those two great commands of which Jesus reminded us.

Let's try to love each other. To be there for each other, and to accept God's gracious gifts for our lives here.

Blessings,

Barbara Phinney

QUESTIONS FOR DISCUSSION

1. In the beginning, Kristin decides to disobey Jackson and continue her search for her mother. Is it proper for her to do so? Would you, under the same circumstances?

2. Early on, we learn Zane has no time for God, having been abused as a child by a so-called Christian. How would you minister to such a person?

3. To protect ourselves, we sometimes avoid things that may lead to pain, as Kristin avoided seeing her parents' crash site. They can become superstitious. Even in our walk with God, we can be superstitious. What do you do that is similar? Do you think it will make God act differently?

4. At the lake, Kristin suggests that Zane ask God to teach him what He wants Zane to know. Have you ever done that? Have you ever asked for wisdom, or a change of heart?

5. Do you agree with Kristin's motives to continue her search? She feels that she owes it to her mother who'd saved her life, and she has no one in her life right now. Would you do the same thing?

6. How do you perceive Kristin? Is she strong, weak, tearful or immature? How would you be in her circumstances?

7. Because He'll never force Himself on anyone, God wants us to take the first step. Zane did that at the lake. Have you taken that first step by asking the Lord into your heart? Or admitting your sin? If yes, do you remember that time? Try to describe it in words.

8. Kristin ministered to Zane without ever realizing it, just by her faith. By combining your own faith with learning to describe concisely your first step toward the Lord, do you think you could become an effective minister for the Lord?

9. Like Zane, are you a bit rusty in your prayers? How can you remedy that? Do you think it would help your life to pray more often?

10. Zane recognized that Kristin possessed a peace he didn't have. How can we get that peace?

11. Zane's parents were not good examples of Christians and they tainted his view. How many people do you know have such an opinion because of people like Zane's parents? Do you have that opinion yourself? How can it be repaired? How did Zane repair his opinion?

12. Afraid she is losing Zane when his brother arrives, Kristin wonders if God was telling her to stop her search. How can we avoid misinterpreting God's will in our lives?

13. Do you get mad at God? Is it okay to argue with Him?

14. Kristin and Zane realize that God is working in their lives when she drops the tissue at his office. Only then was Zane able to see the bomb. Do you see God working in your life in what may seem at the time like a mundane thing?

*Eloise Hill fled the Witness Protection Program
more than twenty years ago, leaving her baby
in the care of rookie FBI agent Jackson McGraw.
Now, knowing the Mob is after her again,
Jackson has to get to Eloise first.
Read on for a sneak preview of*
RISKY REUNION *by Lenora Worth,
the exciting conclusion to the*
PROTECTING THE WITNESSES *series.*

Jackson McGraw stood back as the door creaked open about an inch. Flashing his badge and I.D, he said, "Eloise, it's Jackson. I have to talk to you."

He heard an intake of breath, then the door swung back.

And he took in the sight of her, her eyes wide with shock and fear, her skin pale as she tried to find air.

"Eloise," he said, reaching for the door.

She swayed, her eyes fluttering, her head dropping.

Jackson stepped inside and caught her before she passed out.

"Eloise, it's going to be all right."

She felt tiny in his arms. She looked almost the same, older but still beautiful in spite of the jagged white scar bursting through the pale skin near her lips and the deep circles of fatigue underneath her eyes. And she was still afraid. Her whole body began to quiver with a gentle shaking as she held on to him.

Slamming the door, he helped her to the couch, and looked into her eyes again. They were brown instead of the vivid green he remembered, but the colored contacts matched the rich brown of her long straight hair. Contacts might change the color of her eyes, but he didn't care. That look of fear mixed with disbelief and a bit of wonder broke Jackson's heart and made him even more determined to protect her.

Can Jackson keep Eloise safe
from the danger that surrounds her?
Pick up RISKY REUNION *by Lenora Worth,*
available in June
from Love Inspired Suspense, to find out.

Love Inspired®

Bestselling author

JILLIAN HART

brings you another heartwarming story
from

THE GRANGER FAMILY RANCH

Rancher Justin Granger hasn't seen his high school sweetheart
since she rode out of town with his heart. Now she's back, with
sadness in her eyes, seeking a job as his cook and housekeeper.
He agrees but is determined to avoid her...until he discovers
that her big dream has always been him!

The Rancher's Promise

Available June
wherever books are sold.

Steeple
Hill®
LI87601

www.SteepleHill.com

LARGER-PRINT BOOKS!

GET 2 FREE
LARGER-PRINT NOVELS
PLUS 2 FREE
MYSTERY GIFTS

Love Inspired.
SUSPENSE
RIVETING INSPIRATIONAL ROMANCE

Larger-print novels are now available...

Love Inspired®
SUSPENSE

TITLES AVAILABLE NEXT MONTH

Available June 8, 2010

END GAME
Big Sky Secrets
Roxanne Rustand

RISKY REUNION
Protecting the Witnesses
Lenora Worth

TROUBLED WATERS
Rachelle McCalla

SABOTAGE
Kit Wilkinson

LISCNMBPA0510